WOLVES & GIRLS & OTHER DARK GEMS

WOLVES & GIRLS & OTHER DARK GEMS

MARIA HASKINS

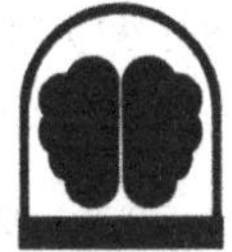

Brain Jar Press
PO Box 6687
Upper Mt Gravatt, QLD, 4122
Australia
www.BrainJarPress.com

Images: *Howling wolf on rock with bird flying around*, Tithi Luadthong/Shutter stock

ISBN: 978-1-922479-59-4 (Ebook) | 978-1-922479-50-1 (Paperback)

CONTENTS

Brain Jar Press
PO Box 6687
Upper Mt Gravatt, QLD, 4122
Australia
www.BrainJarPress.com

Images: *Howling wolf on rock with bird flying around*, Tithi Luadthong/Shutterstock

ISBN: 978-1-922479-48-8 (Ebook) | 978-1-922479-50-1 (Paperback)

INTRODUCTION

E. CATHERINE TOBLER

In my early editorial days, flash fiction was often the bane of my existence. I didn't yet know what I liked, even if I had very firm ideas about what I *didn't* like. A short read was fine, but often felt lacking. Flash stories rarely had full plots—maybe they weren't meant to—but I found myself wanting them to. I wanted characterization, I wanted a journey, I wanted something more than a feghoot. It took some searching, but I eventually found the kind of flash that spoke to me, and one of the writers excelling in the form was Maria Haskins.

Maria always seemed to have a short piece for easy reading on the go. When I wanted to escape from editorial reading and re-engage my creative brain, I could be certain Maria would have something perfect.

Writing flash is a very specific ability—not unlike being able to write a short story that doesn't spin off into novella territories or leave a reader wishing for the novel version to answer all the questions the author didn't. Ideally for this reader, flash is a whole, satisfying story in one bite-sized portion. It should raise a question, it should offer a solution, it should leave the reader satisfied, troubled, refreshed. It should evoke an emotion.

Maria is an expert when it comes to discomfiting a reader. In the best possible way, she can make your skin crawl. She can make you cry your eyes out—in a thousand words or less. This book collects a lot of Maria's work from *The Word Count* podcast, which is no doubt where I first encountered Maria's work.

But which came first?

Having read so many Maria Haskins stories, I no longer remember which came first. It has been a journey filled with cannibals, ghostly sisters, and trains; a map riddled with penciled notes, some locations warned against, others starred and well-worn; a book so well-read, the spine threatens to give way, but when it does, there's another story hidden in the signatures.

Though I don't remember which story was first, I remember being hit by the voices in Maria's stories, and I remember thinking *I hope she submits something to* Shimmer *soon.* And then she did.

Exploring Maria's writing as an editor second was a blessing, because I already knew and loved her work as a reader. Now we had only to cross our fingers and hope that something she wrote would be perfect for *Shimmer*'s pages. "Hare's Breath" (collected in *Six Dreams About the Train and Other Stories,* Trepidatio Publishing 2021) was that story, the ideal blend of love, mystery, and heartbreak. When *Shimmer* closed, I didn't think I would have the opportunity to work with Maria again—but the world moves in mysterious ways, and I guest edited an issue of *LampLight,* which published "A Blank Space Where She Ought to Be," collected here.

If you haven't read Maria's work yet, this volume is a perfect starting point. These stories can be consumed like the candies they are. The world being how it is, maybe you only have time for a quick read before bed; this book will give you that. Maybe you want to slip in and out of a fairy tale on your lunch half-hour. This book has you covered. Maybe you're looking for a guide about how to live as something more than just flesh and bones—there's something else there, you've felt it, and you're wondering: wolf or girl?

This book will guide you.

WOLVES AND GIRLS

"The wolf always dies. The girl always lives."

That's what Dad tells Gwen when he closes the book of fairy tales, right before the story ends. Then he tucks her into bed, and no matter how Gwen pleads, he never reads the ending. She knows it can't be as easy as a dead wolf and a living girl. Nothing is ever that easy, especially not for wolves and girls.

There is only Dad to read her stories and tuck her in. Gwen has no mom. Hasn't had one for as long as she can remember.

"She left," Dad tells her. "She couldn't live here anymore, so she went away."

"Couldn't she stay, for my sake?" Gwen asks, kicking the legs of the table, pouring syrup on her griddlecakes at breakfast.

Dad shrugs and says that sometimes it's better to leave than to stay and become something you don't want to be.

· · ·

In the cedar chest in Dad's room, Gwen finds the only thing Mom left behind: a red cloak, hooded, that smells of flowers and snow. She hugs it close, feeling the soft woolen weave against her skin, feeling the absence of the body that is not inside.

"Why would she leave without her cloak?" she asks.

"Too many bad memories left in the pockets," Dad answers without looking at Gwen, even though the cloak has no pockets.

Dad is a good dad. He can braid hair and mend socks and do laundry as well as any mom. He's not always home at night, though. Sometimes he leaves Gwen alone with the door locked from outside, and the moon hanging clear and bright in the window. He leaves his clothes behind, too. They're laid out on his bed, and in the morning, he wears them again.

"What's so bad about wolves?" Gwen asks, poking at the boiled potatoes and mutton on her plate.

Dad is a good cook. A good hunter too, even though he doesn't even own a rifle or a bow.

"Wolves always die. Better to be a girl, because the girl..."

"...always lives," she finishes the sentence for him.

By the time Gwen is twelve, she knows what Dad does when he leaves the house at night. She's seen him go and come back, she's seen the tracks change from feet and toes to paws and claws beneath the eaves of the forest.

"Is that why mom left?" she asks one morning when the moon has set.

"No."

"Did you kill her?"

"No. She left because she had somewhere else to be."

"What place would be more important than me and you?"

Dad doesn't answer.

Before Gwen turns sixteen, she's realized that maybe it's not that Dad doesn't *want* to tell her the answer, but that he doesn't *know* the answer.

By now, she's well acquainted with restlessness and hunger, and some nights she's the one who stays out late, and Dad's the one waiting for her to come home.

"Everything all right?" he'll ask before she goes to bed.

"The girl always lives," she'll say.

One February night Gwen comes home with her clothes torn and a split lip. The same night, a boy in the village beyond the forest comes home bruised and blinded in one eye.

Dad doesn't ask Gwen if she's all right. He cleans the cuts and mends her clothes. He puts her to bed like when she was little, and he reads her a fairy-tale.

"Read me the ending this time," Gwen says.

"The wolf..."

"No. The *real* ending."

Dad looks out the window at the moonlight on the snow.

"Once upon a time, there was a girl in a red cloak walking through the forest. She met a wolf and followed him home. They loved each other and their baby very much. One night, the girl walked into the woods and disappeared. The wolf tried to find her, but he never did. The wolf thinks that the girl was a red rose in the snow: out of place, but lovely and true in every way that mattered. That's the story. I don't know the ending."

The following night, the villagers come. A full moon hangs low over the trees when they march up to the house, and the dark forest is threaded through with silver and shadows. At the front walks the boy with a bandaged eye.

The villagers have brought fire and knives and rope.

"Stay inside," Dad tells Gwen.

She stands at the window and hears the shouting, hears the door close and lock. The moon shines so bright into the room it blinds her, she cannot see what happens, cannot see Dad turn from one thing to another, can only hear the shrill cries, the snarl and growl, the bones cracking, before everything goes quiet.

She's not sure how she gets outside. Perhaps she breaks the glass and jumps out through the window. Perhaps she breaks down the door.

Dad is on the ground. The men and the boy who came with rope and fire are there, too. They are dead, but Dad is not. Not yet.

Gwen strokes the lingering warmth of his grey and shaggy fur, her head resting on his heaving chest. She feels every ragged breath and heartbeat in his body. She sees the fur turn back to skin, the fangs change to teeth, the paw she holds stretch into a hand again.

"The wolf always dies," Dad whispers.

She knows what he wants her to say, but it's hard to speak the words.

The moonlight shines into her, threading silver and shadows into her flesh, and she feels a familiar grayness stir beneath her own skin, yellow-eyed and red-tongued.

"The girl always lives. But what if you're wolf *and* girl, dad? What then?"

Dad doesn't answer. Perhaps there's no answer to be had. Because nothing is ever easy. Especially not for wolves and girls.

AFTER THE FALL

There are things that happen to you when the blessing of whatever god you served wanes, and your previously immortal body gets stuck in mortal-mode. Things no one warns you about. Like aching joints and the flu. Like hangovers and menopause. Like mammograms. No one warned me that one day, I'd be standing in a non-descript clinic near the local hospital, where a quietly professional and capable woman would squeeze my breasts flat to take pictures of the tissue inside.

But here we are. Here I am.

I don't really mind. I've had worse things done to me. But as I get dressed afterward, I'm thinking that aging, even when it's slowed down and dragged out over centuries, is not for the weak of heart.

"Your doctor will call you if there is anything," the young woman at the reception desk says when I leave.

I nod, put on my worn leather jacket, and head outside.

I already know the doctor will call. I already know what the scan will show. I've already felt it. The lump is small but it's there, waiting to kill me.

Squinting in the spring sunlight, I get into my car and start driving.

Maybe this really is what will finally kill me, I think as I turn onto the highway. I can almost hear the Norns laughing as they spin my thread and ready the shears.

I survived Surt's fire, the ice of Niflheim. I survived the claws of the wolf and the jaws of the dragon. I survived when Asgård fell to ruin. I survived every useless battle I threw myself into after that, wielding whatever weapon was given to me—spears and swords and axes, muskets and pistols. But eventually, when the blessing the High One had bestowed on me faded, I found another kind of life. Quieter. Slower. Safer. Or so I thought.

I've always fought, one way or another, but maybe it's time to go. To let go.

Death's no stranger to me. I reaped so many souls as they shook loose from their armour and their bones, carried them with me to the Halls, to the Fields, to Glory. That's what they called it at least. But where will *I* go when I shrug out of this body? Maybe it's time to find out.

I park the car at the trailhead and walk in between the trees. Here, spring smells like it always did. Earth stirring beneath old leaves, new leaves stirring in the branches. Deep inside the park there's a clearing where the ground is covered in pale, purple flowers. A small path threads its way around the dell, but no one's here except an old man feeding the grey sparrows and the fat pigeons, a bottle in a brown paper bag beside him on the bench.

I walk out into the clearing and lie down. I breathe slow, eyes closed, and feel as if I might sink into the earth. Maybe I could. Maybe I should raise a barrow over myself, fall asleep, and not wake again. Maybe that's what my sisters did, wherever they are now. Hrist and Sigrún, Sváva and Kára, Mist and Skeggjöld.

I miss them.

When I first realized my body was aging, I stopped fighting and got a job. Just odd jobs at first. Waiting tables, cleaning dishes, serving drinks. Eventually, I took a job in a hospice. Thought it would be the place for me, used as I am to death and dying. But it was harder than I thought, seeing all those souls slipping away, not being able to guide them. I've worked in morgues and funeral homes since then, where there is naught but bones and flesh, fare for ravens and wolves, or the incinerator and the coffin as is more common these days.

In the sunlit dell, surrounded by flowers, I drift. I remember Tyr's hand, torn off as the wolf snapped its maw shut. I remember the scent of Idun's golden apples as they shone on the branches of the tree. I remember singing with my sisters as we rode the skies, our voices high and clear like water and ice and sea. I remember the High One, the way he smiled that day he gouged out his eye and sank it in the well below the roots of the ash-tree.

My life is a deep, dark well of time and I drift, sink, plummet. Maybe I fall asleep, because the croak of a raven wakes me, and the old man with the brown paper bag is crouched beside me. A pair of old glasses are perched on his nose, one lens cracked so I cannot see the eye behind it.

"Hild," he says, his voice rough with drink and years.

No one has spoken my name, my *true* name, for an age and more. Hearing it, hearing *him*, makes me shiver, but not from cold nor fear.

"Where are you going, Hild?" he asks. "And would you not rather go with me?"

I look away. I think of the diseased tissue, the lump inside me, waiting to kill me.

"I think I'm dying," I say.

He chuckles. "I thought I was *dead*. Maybe we're both wrong."

I shake my head. "I'm old. I'm sick. I'm…"

"We've lived through worse," he says and takes a swig from the bottle before he offers it to me.

I hesitate, but I drink. The label says vodka, but the drink tastes of sun and spring and Idun's apples. It tastes of *home*.

"What need have you of me?" I ask, as the warmth of the draught flows through me.

He removes his broken glasses, turning his one hale eye to the skies.

"Maybe there's a battle coming," he answers. "Maybe the serpent beneath the world has finally gnawed through the roots of the tree. Maybe it's time to fight again."

In the sky above, storm clouds are gathering, and I hear the rumble of thunder and hooves, the clash of lightning and spears on shields. I hear women, singing as they ride, their voices clear as water and ice and sea.

A BLANK SPACE WHERE SHE OUGHT TO BE

It's 8.30 AM on a Monday, and Tess is hiding in the bathroom again, pretending she's getting ready for school. Mom's roaming the kitchen and the hallway, probably sipping her second coffee, maybe looking for her phone, likely getting ready to yell at Tess.

The bathroom is small and dingy with white cracked tiles above the tub and a worn, beige vinyl floor. It smells of the Lemon Lysol that Mom uses to clean it every Saturday, and of the pink Dollar Store potpourri she keeps in a glass jar on the counter. Tess breathes in that cloying scent, breathes it in deep. It smells like every day of her life: cheap, familiar, inescapable.

"Fifteen minutes!" Mom calls out, right on time.

As if she thinks Tess has forgotten. As if it's not the same every day. As if Tess doesn't stand here in front of the mirror every morning trying to make herself disappear, trying to think of what to say, what to do, so she doesn't have to go. *I'm sick. I'm tired. I got my period. Don't make me. I don't want to. Please, mom.*

But words are useless, just like Tess.

Tess pulls at the sleeves of her hoodie, making sure her

arms and wrists are covered, and thinks of school. The mind-shattering sound of the final bell when she runs from Mom's car and ducks inside the entrance. The rough feel of the stucco wall against her back at recess. The corridors and the classrooms, too bright and too loud. The people, too bright and too loud. The kids, the teachers, the counsellor, the janitor, the receptionist. All of them looking at her as if they know who and what she is, as if they've already decided she's not good enough and never will be. Their ever-present eyes and voices, sharp like shards and splinters, slicing through her.

Mom taps on the door. "Ten minutes. You have to be ready."

Tess doesn't move. Doesn't make a sound.

"Tess?"

"Yeah."

"Ok."

Tess turns on the tap and pretends to wash her hands. For a moment, just an instant, really, her gaze slips off the sink and into the mirror where her own useless face stares back at her.

She has never liked mirrors. Not just because they show her useless face, but because the glass is like the surface of a lake, depths unknown, concealing whatever lurks below. You have to stare into the glass for a long time before you glimpse it, and then you might catch the shadow of its passing, the quiver of its wake, the viscous movement as it almost, almost but never quite, breaks the surface.

"Tess, are you ready to go?"

Tess feels her voice turn into a razor, "Leave me alone. Can't I even go to the bathroom without you bugging me?"

Mom mumbles and walks away.

Tess closes her eyes. She wishes she were somewhere else. Or even better, someone else. Someone who fits in. Someone people *like*. Someone who can talk to others without saying the wrong things. Someone who can laugh without laughing at the wrong bits. Someone who isn't always too quiet or too loud. Someone who isn't the one people always whisper about.

She opens her eyes and forces herself to hold her own gaze in the mirror.

A long time ago, maybe it was grade three, at a birthday party, back when she was still invited to things like that, when she still went, she stood in another bathroom with a group of girls and someone turned off the light and said, *let's do it, let's say it, three times, let's see what happens, if we can see her.*

Everyone else knew the words but Tess didn't. Everyone else spoke the words but Tess didn't. Everyone else screamed at the end when the lights came on and said they'd seen her— Bloody Mary, right there! her face, her mouth full of fangs, her lips dribbling blood—but Tess didn't. Even so, she did feel the presence of *something* that day. Has felt it every time she's looked into a mirror since. Something, waiting out of sight, just beneath her reflection. And ever since, she's wondered what might surface if she stares at the glass long enough.

"Tess." Mom's voice, exasperated now, getting ready to shout. "I'll be in the car."

"OK."

She listens to Mom's footsteps, holding out for a few more seconds before she turns to go, but the moment her eyes slip off the mirror, the bathroom light goes out, plunging her into darkness. Tess stumbles into the door and grabs the handle. It won't budge, even though she's unlocked it. She tries again, jiggling the handle, but the door remains shut.

"Mom!"

Nothing. No reply and no light, except the hair-thin sliver at the bottom of the door, illuminating nothing.

Tess puts her shoulder to the door and pushes, she thumps on it with her fist, but it only makes a dull, muted sound.

"Mom! The door won't open!"

Still nothing. All she can hear in the silence are her own breaths, quick and shallow, and her pulse, pounding in her ears.

Tess retreats into the bathroom.

In the dark, above the sink, the wide, blank screen of the mirror waits for her, its surface shivering with shadows. Tess shivers too.

Let's do it, let's say it, three times, let's see what happens, if we can see her.

The whispers in her head sound like the girls at the birthday party all those years ago. Impossibly, the rising dread at the back of her throat tastes the same too: regurgitated Cheetos and 7 Up. The room feels suddenly too small, its cracked tile walls and beige vinyl floor closing in around her, the Lemon Lysol and potpourri-scented air clogging her nose. Tess closes her eyes and grabs hold of the sink, trying to calm herself, but when she opens her eyes, the door remains closed, the room remains dark. And when she opens her mouth, she speaks the words, even though she did not mean to.

"Bloody Mary."

Her voice is surprisingly firm and loud, and the mirror seems to tremble at the sound of it—like a portal, like the surface of a lake hiding untold depths beneath. Tess reaches out, half expecting her hand to slide through, but there's only glass, smooth and hard.

Say it.

This time, the whisper in her head sounds like Mom, or maybe it's her own voice.

"Bloody Mary."

Tess speaks the words again, and unlike in grade three, there are no shrieks and giggles outside or inside, only hissing whispers, or maybe that's just the rush of blood through her own veins. Her breath hitches in her throat as the darkness collapses around her, folding in upon itself, shrinking to the size of a coffin, a grave, a straitjacket. Tess stares into the mirror, straining to see her face, but the darkness has erased her features, turning her reflection into nothing but a mask: a blank space where she ought to be.

"Say it."

This time, the voice is not inside her head, but inside the room, right behind her, as if someone's leaning close to whisper. Tess wants to scream, wants to call out for Mom, but she doesn't. Instead, she lets her mouth speak the words a third time.

"Bloody Mary."

The world seems to stop and hold its breath. Even Tess's heart slows and stutters, and then... Nothing. No muffled laughter, no furtive whispers, no shrieks and hollers, no apparition, either. Tess tries the door, but she's still locked inside with her own shapeless form waiting in the mirror and the silence closing in around her, stripping her bare of hope and pretense.

Tess inhales the smell of her life, of Lysol and potpourri. She inhales the silence and the darkness. She inhales her fear and loneliness, her anger and pain, until there's nothing left. What she should do is try the door again. What she should do is call out for Mom. What she should do is bust the goddamned door down. But she doesn't do any of those things. Staring into the blank space where she ought to be, Tess knows why. Because she doesn't want to. Because she doesn't want to go out there. Because she wants to stay in here, where even the mirror doesn't know who she is.

Tess exhales, and her breath is cold as ice as it hisses out of her throat, as it unspools over her tongue, as it slips between her teeth, as it is expelled into the darkness. She stares, unblinking, into the dark mirror until she finally sees it: the shadow of its passing, the quiver of its wake, the viscous movement of it as something breaks the surface.

As suddenly as the light went out, it comes back on—vivid-bright and blinding. In that sudden glare, the bathroom looks the same, but Tess's point of view has shifted. She is no longer standing at the sink. Instead, she is looking at the room from inside the mirror, as if through a window. The bathroom isn't empty, though. There is someone out there, standing where Tess stood before. It looks like a girl but her face is as blank as a malfunctioning TV-screen—a featureless, eyeless, mouthless mask of static.

The girl leans closer to the mirror, to Tess, until their foreheads touch. Tess is held in place by the glass of the mirror and sees her own features ripple over the other girl's face, steadying as the static fades, becoming a true reflection of herself, impossible to tell apart.

From inside the glass, Tess watches as the other girl opens the door, as she steps over the threshold. Tess sees the familiar hallway, a glimpse of daylight as the front door opens, she even hears Mom calling out from the car, telling Tess to lock the door, her voice far away and fading.

Tess hears her own voice from outside, hears her own laugher, too, hears the car starting, hears it drive away, and she knows that this new Tess will make Mom laugh rather than scowl on the way to school. This new Tess won't hide in the bathroom every morning, either. She will know how to talk to people. She will know what to say and when to laugh. She will do all these things, and more, so Tess won't have to.

Tess would smile if she could, but inside the mirror, everything is fading.

Tess's own features dissolve, until her face is as blank as the touch of cold glass against her forehead. Her memories wane and dwindle. The smell of pink potpourri and Lysol linger for a moment before they vanish, too. She holds on to her name a moment longer—the fading sound and feel of syllable and letters, the trembling of the air shaped by lips and tongue.

Finally, she lets it go and her name evaporates, like the wisp of a distant cry in the dark; like a warm breath caught on cold glass and she knows it won't summon her no matter how many times it's spoken, because it doesn't belong to her anymore.

SCENT

Her cabinet is full of perfumes, and the scents try to escape as soon as I open the door—twined tendrils reaching out—each scent a murmur, a ripple of memory beneath my skin. There are liquid amber and fluid gold, swirling ruby and molten jade, lustrous indigo and glossy lilac—gleaming prisms of crystal and glass, stoppers carved into birds and beasts and blossoms —all aglow in her gloomy boudoir, lit only by the flames beneath the copper cauldron in the other room.

"Don't touch, Alynna."

Mother's voice. Not loud or sharp, because Mother never raises her voice. But firm. Like the hand on my shoulder, turning me around, away.

She asks me to brush her hair, as she has done every night for as long as I dare remember. I unravel her waist-long braid, brushing black tresses into silk and shadow, her skin already warm and flushed in the heat and steam rising from the deep basin cut into the stone floor.

The golden mirror holds Mother's reflection. She is so beautiful that it hurts even me to look at her: beauty like a blade—a sleek, perfect edge—sliding through skin and ribs so easily you barely notice when it stops your heart. I don't want to look, but I inhale her scent with each sweep of the brush: the smell of spring mornings in the garden, days when she'd hold my hand, bedtimes when she kissed me. Each brushstroke tangling into memory.

Don't touch.

In the other room, the fire keeps the water boiling, heating the large transparent sphere suspended on its chain above the cauldron. Inside the glass, the heated fluids rise, trickling slowly through twisting tubes of copper, dripping into vials. Something twitches within the steam and mist and glass. I do not wish to see. Not tonight.

She rises from the chair, and the weakest part of me wishes that she would stay this way: that she would not undress, not step into the steaming water, not wash and rinse her skin. I breathe in her scent, trying to hold on to it, keep it safe, forever. Mother, safe, forever.

The gown drops, embroidered silk blazing blue and black like butterfly wings, smooth brown skin beneath.

Through the window beyond her naked form, I glimpse the forest: trees, the moon, narrow trails made by paws and hooves beneath shriveled leaves and twisted boughs. There is a way through the shadows and the mires. Maybe a bird could fly above. Maybe a wolf could find the trail. But I have no wings, no fur, no beak, no snout. I have only a child's hands, scarred and calloused. Strong enough to carry water and light the fire, to brush Mother's hair, and lay out the gowns upon the bed. Not strong enough to break open locks or crack the wood that bars the door.

Don't touch.

Once, I touched. Once, I balanced on a stool, reaching into the cabinet, my hand trembling so it almost knocked the bottles over. I took the vial on the highest shelf, in the farthest corner, the one with the carved onyx stopper, wings spread in flight, black feathers carved into the stone. I removed the stopper, didn't let the liquid touch my skin, only breathed: felt the shiver of beak and flight.

That bottle isn't there anymore. Perhaps it's locked in the chest next to her bed, buried beneath pearl-embroidered lace and silver-stitched brocades.

I watch her descend into the scalding water, watch her wash Mother off her flesh and bones with oil and soap and sponge, shedding scent and memories, skin and spirit, until she is twisted spines and cracked hide, gut-rip claws, and needle fangs, red tongue flickering between. The water fills the crooks and crevices of her body, rinsing warped limbs stitched together by sinew, spell, and shadow. She rises, stripped of all illusion. Clean. Strong as roots and vines, as tooth and bone.

In the other room, the glass sphere glistens, tarnished with dark residue above the roiling water. I smell wolf tonight. By now I can tell the smells apart: the animals and birds, the children, the women and the men, the tiny faeries with wings of spun gold, the beasts of horn and wing and tusk. Each trapped inside the sphere, above the heat; giving up its scent and spirit, releasing the essence hid within as the bonds of life are loosened. Only the dregs are left behind, slick and foul, to scrub and clean, leaving my palms and fingers raw.

Don't touch.

A crooked talon strokes my hair, slides down my cheek, cutting into skin and flesh.

"Alynna, give her to me."

She takes the bottle filled only yesterday from my hand, contents shimmering like liquid strawberries and honey: the girl with red hair, barely older than I am, eyes like moss and water. Mouth open, but bereft of sound as she lay inside the glass, as the heat drew out every last bit of her. Her essence held in crystal now, a crimson stopper to keep her in her place.

One splash, two, of strawberry and honey. Firm flesh and

creamy skin blushed with fire flows over stripped bones and creaking joints, eyes like moss and water open, red-brass curls tumble down her back.

"You will be gorgeous one day, won't you?" There is a gleam of hidden teeth and darkness as she speaks. "Make your Mother proud."

I think of black feathers stirring, claws and beak, and I nod.

IN THE GROVE

He finds the girl at dusk.

She is standing in the tall, dry grass at the top of the hill, where the winding dirt road bends unexpectedly around an old split oak. In her suntan and sandals and simple white dress, soft like a nightgown, she is just the kind of girl he was looking for. Just the kind of girl he always looks for. The kind of girl who looks seventeen. The kind of girl who looks like she needs help.

Beyond and below the hill, the sea whispers over sand and rock, shadows gathering beneath the waves.

"You need a ride?" he asks, still astride the rental moped he picked up from the village this morning, the smell of summer vacation wafting off him—tequila, sunscreen, tobacco, sweat.

She isn't sure what she replies. Maybe, "come with me." Maybe, "can you help me?" Maybe she says nothing at all. It doesn't really matter what she says, because it doesn't take much to make him leave his vehicle, to follow her into the grass.

A local boy might have wavered, might even have left her

standing there, might have revved his engine and left her in the dust, but he's a tourist and he follows.

She leads the way into the grass, walking beneath trees he cannot see, trees that are no longer there. As they walk, she reaches out to touch the ghosts of gnarled trunks, bends her head to avoid the memory of crooked branches, listens for the rustle of leaves, long gone.

He takes her hand, and she feels the shape of her own hand in his grip, a girl's warm palm and slender fingers, soft skin and blunt nails. It's a weak hand but pleasing to the touch.

"Where are we going?" he asks.

She doesn't answer, only shapes her mouth into a smile and lets him put his arm around her waist. They're almost there. Only a little longer. Only a little farther.

The sky darkens as they walk, cerulean to cobalt, cobalt to indigo, indigo to obsidian.

So much is gone, but the stone remains. It's low and wide, long as a man, its top flat and smooth, its bulk sunk deep into the dry dirt. When she puts her hand on it, the world shivers. He thinks it's her, trembling.

"Don't be scared," he says.

She isn't.

He touches her, gently at first, eager fingers sliding over this web of skin stretched thin and smooth over bones and guts and sinews. She opens his mouth with her tongue, and he tastes of cigarettes and cheap booze, tart and bitter.

He tugs at her dress and skin, pushes her down on the stone, and looking up, through him, through the haze of his quickening breaths, the memory of the ancient grove grows around her, the old oaks looming like they once did, trunks bent in prayer, limbs reaching out in supplication.

He can't see the grove, but then, it's not for him.

None of this is for him.

He whispers in her ear (the words are sometimes different,

but their meaning is always the same), and she answers in a language she's forgotten how to speak in the daylight, each syllable thorny and sweet on her tongue. In the slick moonlight, her shape is so fluid and pliant beneath him that she wonders if he might notice her lack of solid form.

He doesn't. (They never do.)

"What's your name?" he breathes. She doesn't answer. The leaves used to whisper her name to her, the people used to gather and sing it beneath the oaks, but it's been so long, too long.

"It doesn't matter," she answers, not sure what language or what voice she is using anymore.

She could leave. She could leave him, untouched and alone. She could allow herself to fade away. But why should she? She has always been here. This place has always been hers: this grove, this stone, this hill, this oak, these twisting roots beneath the ground. And this hunger, it has always been hers too.

He tries to kiss her again, his blunt fingers tracing the shivering gleam between the surface and what lies beneath, and she holds on to her body for the final, fleeting pleasure of that touch, but the magic is already slipping off her bones like a discarded husk.

When she lets go, he gasps, hands grasping at her shaggy hide; her shifting, ancient flesh spilling through his fingers, as she takes him inside herself one more time, tasting the last tart and bitter drops of him on her long, raspy tongue.

What's your name?

After all this time, she can't remember. All she knows, all that matters, is this shifting skin and flesh, and the hunger, beneath.

SUNLIT SURFACE, DEPTHS BELOW

She watches the children playing in the shallows, feels her pulse skip and quicken.

The girl is fearless. She runs into the waves and dives below while the boy walks in cautiously, until finally he is floating on his back, arms out, a clumsy starfish.

He'd drown easier, she thinks, smoothing out the bright red bathing suit fabric, tugging it in place around her thighs, trying not to feel the hunger twisting in her gut, the craving for flesh and gristle, for tender meat to rip and tear.

Standing here on the beach she feels the weight of her body, so much heavier than it would have been beneath the waves. So slow in this pale, translucent skin. Some days, at home, she feels so slow and heavy it's hard to get out of bed, the weight of what she is and what she can't be anymore, holding her down until she cannot move at all. Those days, life itself seems like nothing but rust and iron, hook and sinker, a body on the rocks, stripped of its lustrous hide.

It's different on the beach, especially now in summer. Easier and harder at the same time. The air smells of salt and seaweed and sunscreen, bodies crowding close in the sand. Gleaming, touching.

She leans on the old merry-go-round: the cracked wood, the sun-bleached plastic of the car-shaped seats. Hears the creaking of the wood, feels the wobble of loose nails and metal bars.

It's been a long time since anyone used the merry-go-round, and the only ones perching on it now are gulls and crows.

She remembers when children played on this merry-go-round, screaming and laughing as they spun. She remembers watching them from the water, wondering what it would feel like to be one of them.

That was long ago.

Everything is long ago.

The sun is hot on her skin, and she stands very still, feeling the hunger, feeling her weight, the lush folds of her waist and belly, breasts, and back.

It's a good a body, but here, so close to the water, she longs to feel the tug of waves and current, to slip beneath and dive until the light isn't even a faint glitter above.

The children play in the shallows. Skin wet and glistening, hair plastered to their skulls.

Nearby, a group of older girls walk by, giggling, tugging nervously at their bathing suits, assuring each other they are beautiful. Nothing weighs them down it seems, and yet she knows it isn't so. Everyone is weighed down by something. Everyone carries their own chain and anchor.

All flesh is beautiful, she wants to tell them, *and beneath the water being round and sleek would serve you well*.

The children scream. She turns, teeth sharpening behind her lips, but they are only splashing each other. Breathing deep, she forces herself to look away. The longing is almost overwhelming now, the desire stirring beneath her skin—to let go, to release herself, to become what she was and should always have been.

She walks closer to the water's edge, heels sinking deep in soft sand, saltwater spilling into her tracks. The strength and power of the ocean lapping at her ankles.

I could leave, she thinks, remembering a day years ago when she tried. When she swam out so far she could barely see the shore, the cold embracing her, fish and crabs calling from below.

The children scream again, chasing each other through the waves. She watches their small bodies cleave the water. Soft limbs, supple skin.

She walks in slowly, relishing the tickle of cold water around her midriff, the gentle caress of waves as they slip inside the red bathing suit. Then, she dives.

Below the surface, her slow, careful movements are transformed into fluid strength. The joy of it almost overwhelms her—her legs fusing as she kicks, nostrils narrowing, pale skin turned mottled grey and black.

Holding on to what she was is like holding a squirming, slippery sea-creature in your hand, its wriggling shape spilling between your tightly closed fingers. It's almost more than she can bear, more than she can stand. She wants to be part of the salty water, wants to dive deep into the darkness, swim up the coast to a beach where the sun plays over smooth pebbles and rippling sand. She wants to feed. She wants to feel raw, fresh meat between sharp teeth, the taste of blood when she swallows.

No.

She's already been under too long, and when she bobs up, she raises her arms slowly to make sure they are still arms, hands, fingers. A shiver of fur and mottled grey slips away along her spine, underneath the bathing suit, her lower body turning back to legs and feet and toes when she closes her eyes and wills it so.

"Wow!" The boy's face is next to hers in the water, brown eyes shining. "You stayed under so long, Mom!"

She smiles at him and rolls over on her back, looking up at the sun.

"Mom, did you see? Did you see me do a handstand?" the girl shouts.

She keeps smiling; keeps her teeth small and blunt, her mouth closed, feels her body lose its fluidity, slowing, steadying. Staying.

"Show me again," she says, knowing that whatever kept her here once, it is no longer *her* body that tethers her, but *theirs*.

It's all right. She can live with it, with the sadness, the loss, buried in her flesh like a barbed hook, she can feel the joy and happiness anyway. After all this time, she knows how to live, knows she can be like the ocean itself, a sunlit surface, hiding the far depths below, seas and caverns full of life and hunger, unseen and unguessed.

THE UNICORN

There's a small hollow beneath a tree near the unicorn's enclosure where Sanguine likes to sit. It's quiet, padded with grass and moss between the roots, and deep enough to hide her from the castle. She likes to come here after lessons or beatings because the unicorn listens to her. Sometimes, she thinks it might even talk to her. It makes Uncle angry when she tells him that. She is too old to make believe, he says.

Tonight, she has brought chocolate for the unicorn. It reaches over the spiked iron fence and eats it out of her hands, its dark velvet muzzle grazing her fingers. Then, it nuzzles her cheek and nibbles at the chain of gold and rubies around her neck.

Auntie says there is no unicorn, only a horse: "It doesn't even have a horn", she mocks, but Sanguine remembers when the animal was brought here. She was very young, and the unicorn was just a yearling: all black-blue-shimmer coat, mane and tail a tangle of spun silver. Its mother was a carcass on a wagon, red blood dripping from black flanks and hooves. Uncle's men had paid dearly for the prize: one limping, one slung over the saddle. The mare's golden horn was stained with blood and gore, and Sanguine remembers that she cried when the men cut it off with an axe.

Treasure, power, magic... anything can be had for a unicorn's horn. But even after all these years, this unicorn has no horn. That makes Uncle and Auntie angry. Maybe that's why they tell Sanguine it's a horse, as if it is the horn that makes a unicorn what it is, nothing else.

The unicorn paws the ground and whinnies softly. It's restless tonight, just like Sanguine.

"Tomorrow," Sanguine whispers. "Tomorrow I must go with the sorcerer."

The sorcerer is young and powerful. Auntie says she should be grateful for such a match, but the man looks at her with a lust that weighs and measures her flesh and skin.

Thick blackberry brambles surround the unicorn's enclosure, twining thorns around the iron fence. Auntie calls the brambles roses and says they are beautiful. Sanguine thinks they are dark horrors, full of rot and shadows. Whenever she looks beneath the brambles, she feels something wriggle at the back of her mind: something long ago, something she can't quite recall.

Sanguine puts her arms carefully through the iron fence, avoiding the thorns, touching the unicorn, and the softness of its hide is like silk and stars and summer nights. It will suffer no one's touch. No one's, except Sanguine's.

Sanguine has tried to believe that the unicorn is a horse, but she can't: even when Uncle laughs at her, even when Auntie strikes her to make her believe. She remembers it so vividly: the blood, the yearling, the dead and injured men, her own tears. She wouldn't remember it if it weren't true, would she? But sometimes that memory shivers, as if something else is concealed beneath it, but she cannot seem to lift that veil.

Heavy boots clatter on rocks. Sanguine pulls back her hand too fast, scraping it on the thorns. She sucks the blood off her knuckles, and there is something hidden in that salty taste, too: something forgotten and forbidden.

Quickly, she crawls into the shadows and rot to hide beneath the brambles; the smell of decay devouring her. Two men with spears. Uncle at the front with his whip.

"I sold one living, and I can sell one butchered. The hide will fetch a good price."

The unicorn rears up, burnished hooves flashing. Sanguine feels its fear and rage as the thorns rip her clothes and skin. A spear prods the unicorn through the fence. It screams. The unicorn screams. *Or did I scream?* Sanguine wonders. Tangled brambles snag her hair and lace and golden chain, the links choking her as she tries to wrench loose.

Uncle cracks the whip and unlocks the gate to the enclosure, and in that same instant the chain snaps and falls off Sanguine's neck.

The spell unravels when the chain falls. Her flesh unravels too. She is no longer girl or niece, she is crawling on all fours, out of the thorns and brambles, flesh and bone twisting and turning as she moves.

"Sanguine!" Uncle's eyes are on her now. She can't answer him, wouldn't if she could, and when the whip cracks again, the world cracks, too. It cracks and falls away, and through the cracks Sanguine can see the world anew: see the garden turn to a mouldering Netherworld boneyard, Uncle's face an undead mask of rage, the castle glowing like a corpse-light, her own limbs turned to four-legs and black flanks.

She also sees the old memory anew. Auntie who is *not*-Auntie, slipping the golden spell-chain over a newborn filly's ears and mane, shifting her, binding her, a treasure beyond horn and hide, right there at her dead Mother's carcass as the yearling is led away. And she sees Uncle, *not*-Uncle, wrench his spear from Mother-mare's chest.

Sanguine shakes her mane, dips her head, neighs as she

charges. The men fall. She stabs not-Uncle through the chest with her exquisite golden horn, breaking the last remnants of the binding-spell when his neck snaps on the rocks.

"There was another unicorn," she says turning to Sister-mare, "and it was me."

FRÄULEIN MARIA

It's late when I push my cleaning cart into the elevator in the basement. Most of the office workers have left the building already, but my shift is only starting. The cart is heavy, loaded with supplies—scrubbers and rags, sprays and polish, broom and mop.

On the main floor, Belinda gets on the elevator with me. She shouldn't be here this late. She works an entry-level, 9-to-5 job in the desert of the open office floor, somewhere in that dreary maze of desks and screens.

"Good evening, Fräulein Maria," she says, clutching a folder to her chest as if it were a shield.

Belinda looks like such a nice girl, all cashmere, curls, and curves, but I can smell the sin on her, beneath that expensive perfume she wears (more expensive than she could possibly afford). It's always in her hair and skin, that stink of vanity and lust. She tries, but she can't ever scrub that stench away.

"Working late?" I ask, peering at her through my thick glasses.

Belinda's laughter flutters like a frightened bird.

"Yes, Mr. Latham needs me for some overtime." She glances at me, then away. "You know how he is."

"Yes," I say. "I know how he is."

My Mama would have had harsh words for Belinda. She was tough on dirt and sinners, my Mama. I try to do God's work like she did, keeping the world clean of sin and grime, but I won't ever be as tough as Mama was.

On the third floor, a man gets on the elevator. Unlike Belinda, he doesn't really see me. Not everyone does. Old women are invisible to many people.

I smell the sin on him too, beneath the whiskey, breath-mints, and aftershave. The reek of sloth and envy is almost more than I can stand, and it's a relief when he steps off on the fifth floor.

Sin is the grime that covers up the glory of God's Creation, and we must do our best to rid the world of it. That's what my Mama used to say. She knew a lot about God and sin, even though she never went to church.

"Evening, Fräulein Maria."

It's Hammond, the bicycle courier—slim and tanned, clad in Lycra. Hammond is a rare one. No smell of sin on them at all. Instead, they smell of air-dried laundry, lemon, and dogs. They are as close to an angel as I've ever met.

"G'night, Fräulein."

I nod and even allow myself a quick smile in their direction when they step off the elevator.

Most people here call me Fräulein Maria. One night, someone heard me singing while I mopped, and asked me if the song I sang was in German. I only smiled, and they took that for a yes. Fräulein Maria has stuck since then. It's as good a name as any. Better than some other names I've known.

There is only me and Belinda in the elevator now. Her hands shake when we get off on the top floor, still holding on to that folder, the smell of her sweat mingling with the scent of sin and perfume.

She's crying.

I know why she cries, of course. I know the things she's done for money. I know she wraps herself in fancy scents and clothes and flawless makeup to make people see her as she *wants* to be seen, but I know what she really is. I know her sin, how deep it goes. And every sinner should be cleansed. But, Mama forgive me, I can't help it, I still reach out and pat Belinda's arm as if I'm here to comfort, not to clean the world as best I can.

Mama always said it was our purpose to do God's work even if God has turned away from us, even if we cannot step into a church without our skin blistering, even if we cannot pray without burning our tongues on every syllable.

Mama's last words were the Lord's Prayer, and she revelled in it, even as it burned her from the inside out.

"You should go home," I tell Belinda.

"I can't. Mr. Latham..."

"Go home," I say again, and this time I use my voice the way Mama taught me. To convince. To compel.

Belinda looks bewildered. Then, relief and fear ripple across her face.

"Thank you, Fräulein Maria."

When she's gone, I open the door to Mr. Latham's office.

He is at his desk, lights turned low, sitting there in his expensive suit with his shirt already unbuttoned in anticipation.

Oh, Mama.... If you could see him, if you could *smell* him, you'd be so pleased with me, even if I'm softer on some sinners than you ever would have been. This building, this city, this *world* is overflowing with sinners, but some are surely worse than others. Belinda is a sinner, yes, but this man reeks of greed and gluttony, of wrath and lust and pride, a vile stink that seeps through the whole building, staining everyone and everything.

"Belinda?"

He looks up and sees me.

I don't think Mr. Latham has ever really noticed me before, but in this moment of reckoning, I let him see me as I really am. With a shrug, I shed my cloaks of invisibility: old, woman, cleaner, human. I shed them all as I straighten my back, flex my limbs and fingers, as I remove my glasses, as I bare my fangs.

The world needs cleansing from dirt and sin, that's what Mama spent her life teaching me, and we must use the powers we were given to serve that higher purpose. God, in their infinite wisdom, made us the way we are, and though society might call us monsters, blood-drinkers, demons, we can still serve the creator if we choose.

Mr. Latham screams and soils himself, but I'll clean up before I go.

MABEL'S PACK

The only thing Mabel is grateful for in this whole messy business of being turned into a dog, is that she turned into a dog that's big enough to break out of the preschool's backyard. She's looked at herself in the mirror, and near as she can figure, she's some kind of rottweiler-lab mix, with a wrinkled forehead that gives her a permanently worried expression.

"What if I was a toy poodle?" she says to the kids while pushing on the three wobbly fence-boards. The kids laugh, though it mostly comes out as howls and barks since they are now a bewildering mix of puppies, toddling around on wobbly legs with wagging tails.

Twenty-four hours ago, she was a preschool teacher, and they were a dozen three- to five-year-olds. Then... Mabel shudders, remembering the vertigo, the queasiness, as her body changed.

She digs her claws into the frozen ground, pushing on the last board.

She wants to go home. Maybe Robert's there. Maybe he's safe.

All day yesterday she kept the puppies inside the preschool and the backyard. She couldn't open the preschool's locked front door and she figured someone would come and help. It seemed a reasonable thing to expect, but no one came. And once she realized what was happening outside, in the street, she was too scared to leave.

First, a group of rhinos ran by. Then, a buzzing cloud of insects passed. After that came the snakes and the toads and the boars. Watching from the preschool window, Mabel somehow knew that all those creatures had been people, just like her, and that they were all crazed with fear and panic now.

She kept the kids busy playing and raiding backpacks for snacks. As darkness fell, she saw fires burning far away, heard distant alarms go off, but still no one came. No police, no ambulance. No Robert.

"What about my mom and dad?" Adrian, one of the five-year-olds, asked before he fell asleep.

Katarina, another five-year old, snuggled close.

"I like you as a dog, Mrs. Winston. "You're a good dog."

This morning when they woke up, seven of the kids had lost the ability to speak. They bark and chase each other through the backyard now, and don't seem to remember that they were children yesterday.

Mabel peers through the busted fence as the last board comes loose, sniffs the cold air, feels her hackles rise unbidden. There are too many scents, too much information to process all at once, but she has to move.

Maybe Robert's home, she thinks. *Maybe he'll know what to do.*

Mabel tries not to think about how far away home is, tries

to think of the calm countryside around the house instead, all the food in the pantry, and the old dog-door they never got rid of after Shadow died. She figures she'll keep off the main roads and bridges, cut across the frozen bay to get there faster, safer.

"Alright," she says, trying to sound jaunty. "Come on! Stay together and be good dogs!"

She keeps the puppies close because even though it's quiet now, the town feels, and smells, *wrong*.

Beneath a tree, a cougar is eating something, guts spilling across the concrete, noisy crows watching from above. The cat turns toward them, and Mabel growls, wondering if the cougar is a real cougar, if the dead thing was a real animal, if the crows are real crows.

It's all real now, she thinks, feeling her insides lurch.

———

It takes longer than she planned to reach the bay and once they get there, the pups are tired. Mabel looks at the ice, the boats stuck in it. Home is on the other side. She can't see it, but she can smell it.

A flock of geese are waddling around near the shore, nibbling in the snow. One goose reminds her of Robert. Part of her wants to bark at it and chase it, but she remains still, trembling.

"Mabel?" asks the goose, peering at her.

"Robert?" She wags her tail.

———

"We changed right in the library," Robert says while the cold wind ruffles his white feathers. "These are the high school kids who were with me. We're heading south."

"Why?"

"Don't know. Feels right. Maybe we'll find help." He hesitates. "Mabel... The TV was on when it happened. The lady on the news from overseas... she... turned into a donkey."

After that, there's not much left to say.

"I'll be back in spring," Robert says. "No matter what."

Mabel looks up at the sky when he takes flight and feels something brittle snap inside her.

It's late. Too late to take the puppies across the bay. They'll have to wait till morning. Only the two oldest, Katarina and Adrian, can still speak, but at least all the pups follow her. They raid the nearby Starbucks, drinking milk off the floor and eating sandwiches. There's no one there, except some large ants crawling over the cookies. Mabel looks at the ants, thinking about all the moms and dads who used to go to this Starbucks for a coffee every morning.

———

That night, she can't sleep. She thinks of Robert, flying south. Of how far-offspring is.

Adrian whimpers next to her.

"Maybe some girl made a wish," Katarina whispers, spaniel eyes gleaming in the dark.

Mabel looks at her; quiet, tail still.

"Most animals are nicer than people," Katarina goes on, and Mabel thinks of Katarina's mother, a loud woman who smells of booze sometimes. She thinks about the bruise on Katarina's arm last week, about the black eye last month. "Maybe the wish came true even though the girl didn't expect it."

"What if we can't speak tomorrow?" Adrian asks, shivering.

Mabel looks through the glass door, across the frozen bay, past home, past spring, past everything.

"Then we'll be dogs," she says firmly, feeling the warmth of the puppies gathered around her. "Then we'll be good dogs, Adrian."

MIRIAM AND CAT

Cat waited for Miriam to get up. He waited a long time, but she didn't rise. She didn't put fresh herring on his plate. She didn't fill his water bowl. She didn't open the back door so he could refuse to go out in the snow. She didn't clean his box, even when he mewled and scratched sawdust all over the rug.

By afternoon, Cat was very hungry.

He walked around the cottage, tail held high and twitching. The sun was going down. Miriam hadn't put any wood on the fire all day, and even the embers had died down on the hearth. It was getting chilly. Already, the frost on the outside of the windows had started to creep inside the glass. The landscape surrounding Miriam's cottage was white, softly folded beneath new snow.

Cat was cold. Miriam was cold too. She hadn't watered the plant on the table, and its single blue flower had begun to droop. She hadn't touched her knitting. The woolen balls of yarn lay abandoned in the basket. Cat could play with them all he wanted, and Miriam wouldn't be there to scold him, but he left them alone. Playing with the yarn was really only interesting if Miriam told him not to.

He curled up on the bed next to Miriam. The sheepskin-throw soothed him, but he missed his warm spot by the fireplace, and his other warm spot near the iron stove. He missed Miriam's calloused, gentle hands stroking his fur. Cat looked at Miriam. She lay very still under the covers. She wasn't moving. She wasn't breathing. He understood that Miriam might not get up to feed him at all today, or any other day.

A long time ago, Cat had been colder and hungrier than this. He'd been wounded and hunted. Some people from the village had chased him through the snow. They had wanted to kill him for his black fur and yellow eyes, but Miriam had let him in.

"He's the devil!" a man had shouted as Cat cowered behind Miriam, nursing a wounded leg and paw. "Mama Jordan's cows have all gone dry, and the Pellers's horse went lame, right after this cat was seen close by."

Another man had raised his voice.

"My Nellie just gave birth to a baby with a red birthmark on its forehead, shaped like a five-pointed star. That demon cat was there when it happened!"

"The cat has to burn!" a woman had shouted.

Cat didn't want to burn. Fire was nice, but not when you were tossed in the flames. He'd licked his hurt paw, hoping he wouldn't get another taste of the pitchfork.

"Go home, the lot of you," Miriam had said, wielding her broom as if to fend them off. "This cat is in my house now. If you want to burn him, you'll have to step inside."

Cat had watched the crowd from behind Miriam's skirt. He had seen the fright on their faces. Someone in the back had suggested they should burn the house with both Miriam and Cat in it.

"You want to try that, Alan Wickers?" Miriam had said, in a friendly voice. "But then, who will make that salve for your nether regions when you get the rash again?" She looked at all of them. "Who will get the fever off your children in the spring? Who will get the little people to leave your barns alone?"

Grumbling, the angry people had eventually left, and Miriam had cleaned the cut on Cat's leg, smearing it with honey and wrapping it in linen. She had served him a full bowl of chopped liver—herring roe on the side—and made a bed for him by the fire from a thick blanket padded with carded wool. Never in all his days had Cat eaten so well or slept so soundly.

He had stayed with Miriam ever since. And now she'd left, leaving him and her body behind.

Cat watched Miriam's face as the darkness gathered outside. A half-moon shone in between the curtains. Cat was thinking. Making cows go dry and horses lame had been fun, at least for the first millennia or so. He'd had some good times giving out birthmarks and making the gargoyles in the cathedrals weep blood once or twice too. But a cat-demon's life was lonely and hard, and you never knew when someone might get the idea to skin you or burn you alive.

Dawn crept through the trees and into the cottage. It touched Miriam's wrinkled face, sparkling in the gleam of white between her eyelashes.

Cat curled up next to Miriam's ear.

"Miriam", he whispered.

There was a sudden rush of heat in the room, as if someone had opened a furnace, unleashing the roar of fires deep below, and then all went quiet. Cat's voice was so hot that a tongue of flame almost licked Miriam's grey hair. Still, he breathed out her name just a little longer than necessary, to get the arthritis out of her joints, too. The flower on the table heard him as well—its drooping stem straightening.

Cat waited. Eventually, Miriam's eyes opened. She coughed. She blinked in the dawn light.

"My goodness, Cat. Did I oversleep? You must be starving."

Cat meowed as pitifully as he could, threading his black body between her legs as Miriam got up and fetched the herring from the bucket out back.

MOTHER'S LOVE

Doctor, thanks for coming to see me and my son. I know things look bleak for him. I know what you said after the surgery. That you wish you could save Ben. That you did everything you could.

Could you sit with me for a bit? It's a lot to ask. You must be tired, ready to go home. I just... need someone.

Thank you.

All day, I've been sitting here by his bedside, useless. Holding his hand. Wishing I could pray.

I don't usually pray. Not really a believer.

Do you mind if I hold your hand? It helps.

Did you know that I saved Ben's life once, about twenty years ago? I've never told anyone about that.

He was ten when the truck hit him. Crossing the street. Didn't look. Neither did the truck driver. I saw the whole thing. Steel and chrome, all that weight. My son, torn apart.

Afterward, the doctors said he wouldn't make it. Just like you told me today when he was brought in after that head-on collision. I sat by his bedside then too. My mom sat beside me just like you do now. Holding my hand.

I didn't believe in prayer, but mom did.

"Melissa, you have to pray," she told me. "Pray to God and he might save Ben."

I wanted to scream at her. Wanted to tell her that God is useless. I mean, if there's a God, why didn't he just stop the truck in the first place? But I didn't say that. Instead, I held her hand while she prayed.

I looked at Ben's face. At the tubes and wires. At the screen that showed his life as blips and graphs and numbers. Mom was crying and praying. I didn't cry. I was just angry and hurting, but finally, I closed my eyes and tried to say something. Something that would make a difference. Like I'm doing now. It wasn't much of a prayer, really. The only words I could think of were "let him live". I thought those words over and over again, like a mantra or a spell. Must have said them a thousand times.

And then, I felt it. Life. My mom's life. *I felt it*. It was like a spool of thread inside her, like I was holding the end of that thread in my hand. In my other hand I felt Ben's life, and that spool was empty, just like it is now. Sitting there, with all my pain and rage burning through me like hellfire, I felt the thread move as I unspooled my mother's life and let it run through me, into Ben.

I'd never done anything like that before, never dared to try it ever again afterward. Until today.

By the time Ben opened his eyes, mom was dead. I let go of her hand just like I'm letting go of your hand now. There. That's better.

You see, doctor? You were able to save Ben, after all.

OWL, GIRL, ROOKS

It's a late winter night the first time Owl sees the girl. Owl is swooping low over the frost-bitten field, listening to the rooks settling into the elms by the river. The rooks are causing a ruckus as they always do at dusk. Noisy wings and noisier squawks rake the skies, but even through the din, the girl's presence captures Owl's attention.

She's just a baby, wrapped in a blanket, being carried into the red house near the edge of the woods, but Owl, who can hear the flicker of a vole's breath through grass and thicket, who can spot the shudder of a field mouse beneath the snow, sees the baby's heart.

Beneath fleece and flannel, skin and bone, Owl spies the small muscle beating warm and wet in her chest. Owl sees something else too. A tiny shadow wrapped around that heart, a flutter of night grasping at muscle and blood.

Owl does not hoot to herald the child's arrival as might have been done in days gone by when people looked for omens and auguries in the skies, but Owl does not forget that murmur of darkness clinging to pulse and breath.

———

The girl grows up in the red house, in a room on the second floor, her window facing the woods. Owl sees the girl through the window almost every night. The sound of her warm wet heart, and the murmur of the shadow around it, are part of Owl's world now, same as the ruckus of the rooks, the rumble from the motorway, and the whisper of rats and mice beneath the trees.

Owl watches as the girl learns to crawl and walk and run in the garden, as she skins her knees, as she builds forts and huts of sticks in the woods near Owl's tree. Watching her, Owl sees the joy and glory, the tears and tantrums of a girl's life. And always that black shadow, rustling at the edges.

———

One night, the girl sits beneath Owl's tree. Owl isn't sure if she's hiding from someone or something, if it's a game or just a moment of chosen solitude, but there is something different about the girl that night. It's not that she's grown taller or that her hair is styled differently. What's different is that the wet, warm sound of her heart is almost muffled by the shudder and shiver of the shadow in her chest.

Listening, Owl thinks of trapped things: rodents squirming in talons, frogs wriggling in a beak, wings beating against bars of bone.

Owl watches as the girl heads back to the house. Watches as the light comes on in her room. Watches as the light goes out.

Afterward, Owl flies to the river, watching as the rooks settle for the night, sheltered beneath the canopy of elms. They are jostling, huddling together, finding safety in each other.

Owl has seen the rooks come and go for a long time. Has seen the flapping and flailing of their wings, has heard the clacking and cawing of their beaks disturb both dusk and dawn, has seen their number grow, year by year.

The rooks do not remember who they were before they settled in the elms. They do not remember how they came to be what they are, but Owl remembers. Owl remembers the first time each rook settled on a branch by this river. Owl remembers where they came from, even if the rooks have forgotten. And, perhaps, when Owl hoots—the sound of it both omen and augury—the rooks might remember too, even if it's just in the flicker of their dreams.

———

It is a cold winter night when Owl takes flight and swoops low over the frost-bitten field toward the red house. The sky is deep with stars, and the light is still on in the girl's window.

Owl listens for the heartbeat that should be there, but the wet, warm sound is almost gone. When Owl settles in the tree outside, the girl is lying on the bed, her cage of ribs shuddering and shaking as the winged shadow wrapped around her heart tries to shake free of bone and blood, tapping on the girl's sternum with its pale rook's beak.

The girl looks as if she's asleep, and Owl knows there have been other nights such as this, when the girl wasn't sure she wanted to wake. Perched in the trees outside the girl's window, Owl thinks of the baby being carried into the house all those years ago, thinks of the faint black wings fluttering around its heart even then.

Owl has lived a long time and is familiar girls and rooks, with life and death. Life is all around Owl, and all around the girl. Life permeates the woods. It's there in every leaf and root, every whisker and wing, and at all times, death is coiled tight, tight around that life.

Owl also knows there are winged shadows in each of us, searching for a place to roost, a place to rest, for comfort and companionship, and inside each cage of blood and flesh, each winged shadow thinks itself alone.

For years uncounted, Owl has seen those shadows break free of breath and bone, shake out their rook wings and find their place in the elms by the river, forgetting what they were. And while Owl has no real opinion on the fate of girls or rooks, the branches of the elms seem full enough, noisy enough, already. Perched on the windowsill Owl hoots—once, twice—both an omen and augury.

Far off, in the trees by the river, the rooks stir in their sleep, dreaming of where they came from and what they once were. Inside the room in the red house, the girl stirs as Owl takes flight, as the winged shadow quiets beneath her ribs, as her wet warm heart continues to beat a little longer.

KAIJU OUTSIDE HOPE

"Mom!"

Allie's voice. I see my daughter's face above me, illuminated in the dark. She's covered in dust, tears trickling through dirt and blood.

Blood?

I try to get up, but my body won't move. It's too dark to see where we are, but it feels like I'm on a bed, and I hear the hum of machinery or computers. Probably a hospital or clinic.

Memories flash by. Glimpses. The alien invasion. Gigantic, voracious aliens pouring through that space-time rift, cities burning, people dying. Earth's armies fighting back with tanks, drones, bombs. Losing. Helpless. Pete and I escaping Vancouver with Allie, heading for the resistance outpost in the Fraser Canyon. Pete, crushed to death by an alien behemoth on Highway 1 outside Hope. Me, watching, helpless. Allie and I on the road for days, death and destruction at every turn. Then, the outpost. Allie, running into the sheltering tunnels ahead of me, aliens close behind. After that... nothing.

But Allie's here, alive. I'm alive.

"Mom? Can you talk?"

I try, but my mouth feels strange. *Talk*, I tell myself.

"I'm...OK. Are you...hurt?"

My voice sounds odd, but Allie smiles.

"I can't believe it. You're back."

"How long was I out?"

"A week."

Week?

"Where are we?"

"With the resistance. But we're under attack. We're evacuating."

I hear shouting and gunfire. The ground shakes. I know what that means: the aliens are close.

Move, I tell my body, and it finally does, but my limbs feel heavy, unfamiliar.

"Careful, mom, your legs... aren't what they used to be."

I stand up. It's dark, but everything in front of me is illuminated. Almost as if the light is coming from me. A headlamp? I touch my head and hear a metallic clang. Looking at my hands, I see four metallic limbs.

"What the...?"

I look down at Allie. Wait, no. That's not right. At fifteen, she's already taller than me. How...

The mechanical hum is close, in my ears. More shouting, more gunfire. Closer. A door opens. Someone shouts, "Allie! We have to go!"

Allie turns to me, dead-serious.

"Remember the news stories, mom? That new plan to fight the aliens."

"Yeah. Something crazy about... putting human brains into indestructible robots and..."

"When we got here, that tunnel collapsed. You..." Her eyes mist over. "You died."

"What?"

"Your body was crushed, but your brain was still OK, and

they asked me if I knew what you'd want, and I said... you'd want to fight."

"What happened to me?"

But I already know. That mechanical hum, that's my body. Servos, power cells, metal joints.

I look at my arms. Two are blasting weapons of some kind, lit up and charging. The other two have steely, finger-like appendages that can grip, or be fused into stabbing blades.

"How do you feel, mom?"

"I feel..."

Strong.

With an almighty crash, an alien blasts through the wall, teeth and tentacles snapping.

My blasters hum. The sound is pleasing.

"Duck, Allie," I say, and fire.

CHIAROSCURO

Ben always slips the coat check girl at the Chiaroscuro Club an extra twenty bucks when he goes there on Friday nights after finishing work at his art studio.

Her name is Lou, and it's not like he thinks the money will buy him anything extra. She's not that kind of girl. But he likes the way she reminds him of Ava Gardner when she smiles, and he likes the way she dresses, too, always in silk charmeuse, impeccable and eye-catching, even in a club where everyone dresses as film-noir as possible.

Tonight, when Lou reaches for his coat, her sleeve rides up revealing an old bruise on her upper arm, violet fading into green.

Ben has seen bruises on her before, scratches too. He asked her once and she said she has a dog. Ben could tell she wasn't telling the truth but hasn't asked again: he just thinks she's the kind of girl who deserves better.

He sits down at the bar with his usual scotch and newspaper. From his seat, he can still see Lou at the coat-check. She's wearing her red dress. Sometimes the dress is black. Ben prefers the red.

Whenever he paints Lou, and he often does, he paints her in the red dress. He's hung a few of those paintings at his gallery shows and they always sell. Sometimes he paints her naked, too, but he knows that's self-indulgent and he keeps those pictures to himself. Yet in all his paintings, he's never quite managed to capture the way Lou *really* looks. There's always something missing, but he can't figure out what it is.

Ben orders a second scotch right away. That's unusual, but he has a present for Lou and figures he needs the extra courage. It's a silver bracelet set with green stones that he found at an antique store. Gold might suit her complexion better, but it's vintage: something she might have bought for herself, he thinks, if she could afford it.

Lou is gone when he downs the second scotch. She always heads out for a smoke about this time, and when Ben slips outside, she's standing on the corner with a cigarette, patting the pockets of her coat.

"Need a light?"

Ben doesn't smoke, but he's carried a lighter since the first time he saw Lou smoking. She has to steady his shaking hands around the lighter because he is reeling from her scent: a heady perfume that clings close to her smooth skin.

"Thank you."

The husky voice, the glinting teeth, and the look on her face when she inhales makes Ben catch his breath.

This close, Ben can see a ragged scar on her left collarbone, peeking out of her décolletage when she crosses her arms. Knife, he thinks, and shudders. Or maybe vicious enough to be a bite.

His fingers brush the scar tissue beneath the silk. He can't help himself. It's her scent, the closeness, that makes him overstep.

Who would hurt you? he thinks, anger and desire tangling deep inside.

Maybe he spoke the words out loud. Lou looks up. Her eyes darken with fear, or pain, or maybe rage. Almost he might believe that there is a hint of fire between her lips, a heat within that has nothing to do with tobacco.

Ben turns. He runs. Runs until he doesn't know where he is. The smell of Lou is still inside him when he stops.

———

That night, in his studio, he paints in a frenzy, and everything is Lou. He wakes up with her face everywhere: pencil, charcoal, oil. None of them are any good. Except one: oil on canvas, chiaroscuro style. Fitting, he thinks.

Lou's face is light and shadow, her body a slip of red, and it is the best picture of her he's ever painted, one that finally captures the way she looks. The only thing marring the perfection is a dog: grey, wolf-like, lurking in the shadows behind her.

Ben knows he can't have painted that dog—he never paints animals. It's almost as if it's crept into the picture by itself while he slept. He hangs the picture on the wall anyway, and for days he cannot paint, cannot work. He puts the painting away, but Lou's eyes, and the dog's, follow him everywhere even so.

———

He stays away from the Chiaroscuro Club for weeks. When he finally goes back it's a Thursday and Lou's not there. Another girl takes his coat.

He wheedles Lou's address from her. It's a house on the worst side of town, surrounded by an unkempt hedge. The gate is rusted, screeching. It's dark. He can just make out the porch and the door. He knocks. Knocks again.

When he turns to leave, Lou is standing just inside the rusty gate, as if she's waiting for him. In the light of the full moon, she looks just like in his painting: shadow and light, slip of red.

"Who is it?"

Her voice is rough and when Ben walks closer, he can see that she is sickly pale. *Like she needs someone to take care of her*, he thinks and somehow that makes him feel better. There's a smell about her tonight, too, but it's sharper, rougher than last time.

"It's Ben. From the club. I...I have something for you. I think you'll like it."

She opens the box. There's a gleam of silver, and then a growl. Ben looks around for a dog until he sees Lou's face.

"Lou?"

"Silver?"

The word twists into a laugh, then back into a growl as everything changes in the moonlight. And when Lou finally embraces him, like he's always wanted, there is no silk, no smooth skin, no gleaming hair. There are only savage claws and ragged fur, as the dress slips off Lou's lupine body and her sharp teeth snap at his throat.

BURIED

I first see you in the library, on the top floor of this old house you're visiting with your parents.

They've come to assess the value of an unexpected inheritance—house, property, money—but a week of wills and lawyers is too boring for a twelve-year-old girl. That's why you're roaming the house alone.

A lonely child. Quiet. Watchful. *Wanting*. Like I was.

Can you feel me watching you, Ellinore? Maybe. But you cannot see me. Not yet.

I can see you. I see you touch the books, their leather-bound spines, caressing gilded letters, dusty covers. I see you walk past shelf after shelf as if you're looking for something.

I know what you're looking for. Don't worry. You'll find it.

There. That's it. Use the chair to reach it, tucked in behind the other books on the highest shelf.

The black leather cover is embossed with letters. You trace them with a finger, stroking the book's soft skin. Supple, isn't it? I won't tell you what kind of creature was skinned to make it. (No one ever missed that boy, anyway.)

You open it, turning the pages, taking in my ornate handwriting, the rusty brown ink.

My own ink. My own quill.

(It was a Thursday in September when I hid my book here in the library. I was in a hurry because Father was coming up the stairs, shouting my name like a curse, feet thumping on the steps. I ran downstairs after hiding the book, into the basement. Locked a door. Broke a window. Too late.

I only wanted to get away. He should have let me go. But he didn't.)

———

I see you reading the book in bed, the words rustling through your mind. My words. My soul, too, because I tucked a little bit of myself between the pages.

You shiver.

I know why you're cold. I'm cold, too.

Don't worry. It'll all be worth it in the end.

———

When you wake after midnight in my old bedroom, beneath the musty sheets, you hear a thumping noise far below —*thump thump thump*—like a telltale heart. You try to convince yourself it's the furnace, the pipes, the floorboards.

I know it's not. So do you.

In the dark, you reach for the book, caressing its cover.

It's whispering to you, and you listen.

Your mouth moves as you read, tasting the words. I know you can feel yourself changing already—just a ripple, just a quiver—but undeniable.

You're falling asleep with the book in your lap, until I tap on the window.

Tap tap tap.

Don't fall asleep, Ellinore. You've been asleep for too long. So have I.

Tap tap tap.

You scream. Your mother comes. I see her try to soothe you.

She looks out the window, looking at me but through me. She cannot see. You can, though: your eyes wide, your mouth a perfect O. Your mother says you're imagining things. She tucks you into bed and pulls the curtains.

I can still see you, of course. I see you huddling under the covers, your soul caught between the lamplight and the shadows just like mine was. I'm so close that I could almost touch that soft black hair of yours, the fragile nape of your neck, the curved bones beneath your nightgown.

You tremble and reach for the book again.

Good girl. Don't stop reading.

———

I watch you change as you read the book, as you speak my words out loud when you think you're alone. Every day, my ink stains your fingers, your tongue, your dreams.

I see you looking at that old photograph of me on the piano. Me, stiff-backed and neatly coiffed, dressed in black. Father hovering behind me as he always did.

I wonder what they've told you about me.

Maybe nothing. A dusty great grandaunt dressed in silk and lace, long gone, silent, childless, wrapped in the darkest folds of family history, slipped into the silence between shame and fear.

There was no hangman's noose for me, no bonfire gathered to burn me alive, though father threatened me with both. I did not care. I learned the words anyway. Spoke them. Let them change me.

You're like me, Ellinore. None of the others are. None of the others were.

I've waited so long for you, for another telltale heart beating unheard.

———

At last, I watch you get out of bed and sneak downstairs into the basement. Your steps are so light, your shadow so thin and wavering, it's almost as if you've already left this body behind.

Thump thump thump.

You know it's not the furnace, the pipes, the floorboards.

I see you searching with your flashlight. I see you hack and dig into that patch of blackened dirt beneath the bricks father placed to hide what he had done.

I know what you're looking for. You'll find it, soon.

Thump thump thump.

It's getting louder. Keep digging, Ellinore.

There. Your soiled fingers touch the iron-bound wood that father slammed shut around me, and you haul it out of the cold dirt, cracking the rusted lock open with the blade of your shovel.

Thump thump thump.

Beating. Like a heart. Like wings.

The box breaks open and, in the silence, you kneel. You caress my body like you caressed the books that first day: stroking the black feathers, tracing the shiny beak, the claws and feet.

"Thank you, Ellinore," I whisper as I slip my spirit inside my raven-hame again, as I feel the delicate rustle of my wings, shaking off the cold, cramped centuries.

And you, you watch me take flight, your bare feet earthbound only for a moment before the feathers shiver down your spine and arms, before you open your beak and caw with me, as we alight, as we break through the glass and wing together into the night.

WOLFMOTHER

Alba has been tracking the wolf since sunrise. It's late morning now as the beast leads her away from the fields and byres of the valley, up into the mountains. Beeches, alder, and rosehip turn into pines and birches as the slopes get ever steeper and rockier.

The sun climbs to midday, but it barely warms the early spring air. Still, Alba does not slow her pace, breathing hard, sweating beneath her worn leather armour and patched red soldier's cloak. The wolf does not slow either. It keeps ahead of Alba, trotting fast and sure back to its den. Even with a belly full of scavenged meat it's moving swift and steady. Whenever Alba catches sight of it ahead, it is a running shadow. A sliver of grey between the trees.

Alba feels the familiar weight of her bow and quiver on her back, of the knives at her belt beneath the cloak. Five years at war after being conscripted. Five years of being forced to serve the king and realm in whatever wars the rich and powerful deemed necessary. Five years away from this valley, away from the homestead, away from her family. And once the five years were done, there was the two weeks journey to make it home from the mud and horrors of the front. And then....

Alba forces the memory aside and quickens her pace, each breath a knife's edge between her ribs.

Yesterday, she knew what she was. A soldier, returning home from war. Daughter. Sister. Granddaughter. Now, she is nothing. Just a tangle of rage and grief.

Alba knows she should feel hunger, thirst, exhaustion, but she feels only a burning purpose: to follow the wolf. To end its life with knife or arrow. To punish *someone* for everything she's lost.

She could turn back. Could leave the wolf to its own devices, but there is nothing behind. Nothing left of what was Alba's life until now. No homestead with Ma and Grandma tending the cattle and garden, no siblings or dogs to greet her, no Pa wiping the sweat off his brow as he looks at her and smiles from the barn. All gone. Looted. Killed. Burned.

Five years. Every day another stitch of pain and longing in the fabric of Alba's life. And then everything she yearned for ripped away while she was on her way home. The deed done by raiders from one side of the war or another.

Anger burns like a fiery brand in Alba's chest, but the guilt is worse. It's a spear, twisted in her heart. That she was not there to help. That death came calling while she was away.

Alba thinks of Grandma's dead body on the threshold and the wolf standing over her, hackles raised, teeth bared, muzzle rusty with gore. She thinks of the ravaged bodies in the yard. Food for crows. Food for a wolf. Alba yelled to make them scatter and they did, but the damage was done. Flesh torn. Bones picked clean. And no one there to punish, only the wolf, come to eat what was left of Alba's life.

Alba follows the wolf as daylight fades. Up the mountain where gravel and rocks slip beneath her feet, and still the wolf stays ahead, revealed only by the mocking gleam of its silver fur, the shadow of its stride.

It gets colder as evening falls, and Alba buttons up the worn red cloak, pulls the hood up over her hair. The sun has almost set when she reaches the crest of a ridge where crows and ravens scatter in the fading light, crying with displeasure. The peaks of the mountain reach up high above her, a jagged edge of rock and snow. Alba does not see the peaks. She sees only the wolf.

The beast is so close now that Alba hears its ragged breathing, but there's a stillness beneath that sound that makes her pause rather than nock an arrow or unsheathe a knife. A smell of rot in the air brings back battlefield memories, nightmares of war, as the noisy tumult of retreating crows shakes loose her grief and pain. Alba sees it, then. Sees the wolf, the world, herself, true at last.

The wolf's belly hangs low, teats long from suckling pups. A wolfmother. Pups not yet weaned. Behind her on the ridge is a den, but the hollow between the rocks has been torn open. Blood and gore streak the ground. Slaughter work. Hunter's work. Killing. Skinning the bodies to bring the hides to town. Leaving the rest for crows and ravens. Whatever pack lingered here, whatever pups and grown wolves called this home, they are gone. All except one.

Wolfmother stands with her head low, tongue lolling. She is a tired beast. Alba feels her own limbs ache and burn from running all day. She is so close to the wolf that she can see every silvery hair on Wolfmother's snout, the puckered scars on her head, the freshly torn ear, the hot breath cooling into mist.

In the setting sun, Alba sees herself as Wolfmother must see her: a tall, young woman in a faded red cloak and worn soldier boots. Body and soul scarred and twisted by war and grief, hunger and rage.

Wolfmother's amber eyes kindle in the last rays of daylight. Alba wants to look away but cannot because something new and unexpected shivers between them as their breaths mingle in the cooling air. An understanding. A kinship. A bond that is new and tenuous, like a slight root tendril when it first reaches from seed into soil. But it is there, and it is undeniable.

Alba's body sags beneath the weight of everything she's lost. Up here, above the world, she is nothing but a hollow bone, and when the cold wind picks up it blows right through her, the sound of it a wordless, keening lament.

Wolfmother's voice joins hers, the fierce edge of a mother's anguish twining about Alba's own rage and sorrow. In the silence that follows, Alba touches the rough silver of Wolfmother's head with cold fingers. The wolf exhales, and the sound is a sigh.

"I know," Alba says and turns to look down at the valley below as day fades into night. The river like a silver ribbon. Fields stitched together by ditches and fences. Roads and trails. Tracks to follow.

Alba knows it might take weeks to find the hunters who skinned the wolves on the mountain. Longer still to track down the raiders who ravaged the homestead. But at least she will not be doing it alone.

HUNGRY BEASTS

"Where are we going?" I ask Daniel again, and once again he smiles from behind the tiller and tells me it's a surprise.

I smile back, nibbling on my potato chips, trying to relax in the May sunshine as the boat skims the waves.

"Don't wreck your appetite, Bethany!" he calls out. "Remember, I'm cooking dinner on board tonight."

Cheeks burning, I put the bag of chips away, even though I'm ravenous.

It's my own fault. I know Daniel doesn't like it when I eat between meals. I should have had a bigger breakfast, but I was afraid of getting seasick and throwing up.

I've never been in a sailboat on the open sea before. Never even swam anywhere but a pool, and even then, my grandma was terrified for me.

"I don't want to lose you," she'd say and hug me tight when I got home, smelling of chlorine.

Strange that being here, with Daniel, should make me think of grandma.

She was so scared of the ocean that she moved away from

the coast with grandpa, settling down half a continent away on the prairies where the only water not on tap was creeks and ponds.

"The sea is dangerous," she always said. And she really believed it. Mom never even learned to swim because grandma wouldn't let her.

Even though I moved to Vancouver a year ago, it never struck me until now that grandma came from somewhere around here. But since she never spoke of it, I don't know where.

Daniel is explaining ropes and wind, but his words slip right through me. Instead, I listen to the ocean whispering beneath the keel. It's just a murmur, and I'm not sure what it's trying to tell me.

Daniel laughed at how nervous I was getting on board this morning. He didn't laugh about the bathing suit though. I wore my old one: flower-print and ruffles, and I knew as soon as I saw his face it was a mistake.

"It's just...you look so much better in the black one I bought you," he said.

I know what that means. It means the black one makes my waist look thinner; my thighs less thick. Just like the dresses he picks out for me. They all nip and tuck. Squeeze and hold.

Always expensive stuff, though. Top-notch.

His food is top-notch, too, even if it always leaves me hungry. There's just never enough of it. Still, it's nice that he cooks. Mom says I should be grateful.

Stomach rumbling, I grab a beer from the cooler and watch the coastline. I wonder if I've seen this place before, in a movie or a photo, maybe, because everything is strange yet familiar: the undulating shape of that mountain range, that rock jutting out into the waves, that inlet cutting through the forest.

Grandma would have known, I think, listening to the plaintive voices of the gulls, calling out long-forgotten names.

"The sea is dangerous because it remembers too much," she told me when I visited her right before she died.

"What does it remember?" I asked, but she never said.

Daniel keeps talking, but I'm leaning on the railing, looking into the sea, and it's hard to hear his voice. It's almost as if he speaks another language, one I don't understand anymore, one I don't want to understand.

———

In the afternoon, Daniel anchors the boat in a cove. The forest crowds close, and on the beach, smooth rocks slip into the waves.

"Look," Daniel says, pointing at the shore, but I've already seen them.

There are three of them, lounging at the water's edge. Their hair is long, twined with seaweed, webbed fingers waving lazily, necks strung with braids of kelp, shells, pearls.

"Can you see them?"

I close my eyes, look again. They're still there. I look up at Daniel, heart pounding against my ribs.

"What...what are they?"

He laughs.

"They're sea lions, dummy!"

I look at the shore, trying to see what he sees, but I can't. I see thick-limbed, smooth-skinned female bodies lounging, their silvery legs outstretched. They smile at me with sharp teeth, lascivious and inviting, as if they already know who I am.

"They come here to gorge on herring and salmon. I've watched them eat, and they just swallow everything whole. Hungry beasts."

"They're beautiful," I say, but something spiky and cold crawls in the pit of my stomach.

————

We eat underneath the stars and Daniel falls asleep while I do the dishes.

Once Daniel's asleep, I pick at the leftover bits of food in the pantry, but there's nothing left that will satisfy me.

Nothing.

In the dim light, I look at Daniel. There are no sounds below deck other than his breathing, and the strange, yet familiar voice of the sea, murmured words lapping against the hull.

I'm so hungry.

I've been hungry all day, and now the hunger shivers beneath my skin, ripples through my gut, trembles sharp and jagged in my mouth.

I lean over Daniel, inhaling his scent, exhaling my hunger.

When his eyes open, he whispers, then screams a name, but I don't stop, I don't listen, and my new claws and teeth keep tearing through him, because the name he screams isn't mine, not anymore.

————

Afterwards, I head up on deck. I can't see the shore or the women in the dark, but I know they're waiting for me.

I climb down the ladder in the stern and slip into the wet darkness. Three shapes approach, their movements sinuous with predatory grace. I see their smiles already, hungry and beautiful, free of regret and remorse. They are singing a new name to me, their scales shimmering with a green and wavering light as one of them pulls me down beneath the surface. I don't resist.

I sink.

I swim.

Grandma was right. The sea is dangerous. It's dangerous because it remembers who you are, even when you've forgotten.

THE MONSTER HUNTER'S LAST LAMENT

I don't know what you see when you look at me. An old man, I guess. Tired. Worn out.

I should probably tell you what I've done with my life.

Been a monster hunter since I dropped out of high school, hunting down all sorts of creatures, in all corners of this continent. Vampires, werewolves, demons... you name it, I've tangled with it. Ghosts and spirits. Shapeshifters of every kind.

It's been a lonely life; I won't deny it. There aren't many of us in this business, though I've met a few others through the years. All of us haunted, or hunted, by something. Most of them started out like me. They lost someone, and after that they were never the same again.

I lost my brother.

I was eight, Rob was ten. We were walking home from the bus stop after the school bus dropped us off. It was winter, so cold it froze your breath, snow blowing around us in the early dusk. One moment he was there right in front of me, and then he wasn't. Nothing but snow blowing across the road and the fields beyond.

After that, I read everything I could find about monsters,

ghosts, magic, all that stuff. Left home and school and the town as soon as I was able. Left with no goodbyes except a slammed door, and nothing but the clothes on my back and the old rusty car I'd bought from the scrapyard. Started searching the roads and byways for monsters to fight and kill, and more often than not, I found them.

I helped people get rid of poltergeists and restless spirits. I cleared abandoned buildings of vampire trash, hell hounds, and hungry ghosts. I banished all kinds of unclean creatures. Took odd jobs when I could, hanging out at diners and motels, eating too much gas station food and drinking too much cheap beer, living by whatever soundtrack was blaring on the radio. Slept rough, lived rougher. It wasn't a good life, perhaps, but it was living.

The few times I told people the truth of my occupation, they usually didn't believe me, or they thought I was crazy or drunk or high. Who could blame them? So, mostly, if I was asked, I said I was a mechanic, a travelling salesman, a drunk, a drifter. People believe lies readily.

Every now and then I met someone who humoured me, who listened. Sometimes, a woman. Sometimes, a man. Didn't matter which. It's always nice when someone listens. Even if it's only for one night. Maybe that's why I'm talking to you, now, here. Because you're listening.

Anyway, the drinking and the hunting, the roaming and the banishing, that's all done with now. I'm done. Been done for a while, but it's taken me a long time to accept it.

I look at my reflection in this window and I see someone who is spent. Hollow. Old. That's what I am. But inside of me, that boy who lost his brother, he's still there, too. Eight years old and scared out of his fucking mind.

I left home and never looked back. And yet I've dreamed about that stretch of road, that bus stop, that day in the snow, every night since it happened. I've seen my brother a million times in those dreams. Sometimes, I see what took him, too. Each time I dream it, I wake up thinking I should have tried to stop it. Even if it meant that I'd be lost too. At least then we'd have been lost together.

I haven't been back here since I left at seventeen, but I stood outside the old house yesterday, staring at the unkempt yard, the sagging roof. Mom and Dad are long gone. Dead and buried. They're not the ones who haunt me.

I fell asleep with a bottle of rye in my car in the driveway, and when I woke up in the half-light before dawn, it was snowing. I got out of the car, and as I walked down the road, I saw someone walking ahead of me. It looked like a boy, but I knew it wasn't.

I kept walking, past the bus stop, across the field, into the grey haze of snow until all there was was snow and wind and the shadow, ahead. When I finally found this school bus, abandoned here God knows when, I climbed in and found my seat, just like I did every morning back then.

I never told anybody the truth about that day when Rob disappeared. Never told anyone that we argued on the bus. It was nothing special. Just same as always. Small stuff. Brother stuff. Never told anyone that I was still mad at him when that shadow leapt at us out of the swirling snow, grasping and fanged and hungry. I never told anyone that I ran away when it dragged him off. And that every night until I left town at seventeen, my brother would come to my bedroom window wearing his torn skin draped over his bones like a cloak, eyes gone black, mouth gone sharp with teeth.

I knew he waited for me out there, so I read about monsters, and when I could, I left.

And now I'm back here where it began, sitting in this old school bus, in my old seat, looking out the window at you. My shadow.

I know who you are. I know why you're here. I know you've been waiting for me.

I don't know if you've heard a word I've said, if any of it matters to you, but I'm sorry I ran away. I'm sorry I didn't try to save you. I'm sorry the last words I spoke to you were words of anger.

I'm sorry I lived.

I've missed you, Rob. And this time, I promise I won't run.

BIG BAD

You wake up, slumped over the steering wheel.

Raising your head, you look through the smashed windshield. It's dark and it's snowing, and you've hit a tree. Your headlights are still on, white light reflecting off the snow. You see the dented hood, the jagged edges of the broken windshield, and everywhere inside the car, blood. It's slick on your hands, on the shards of glass. There's glass and blood in the back seat, too, as if an animal crashed into the car and scrambled around before escaping.

You try to open the door, but the car is leaning on its side in the snow. Cautiously, you clamber across the passenger seat, pushing the other door open with your feet.

Standing in the snow, you try to remember where you are, *who* you are, anything.

Nothing.

On the floor on the passenger side is a flashlight and a shotgun. You realize you know how to use the shotgun as soon as you pick it up, your hands remembering what your mind doesn't. Instinctively, you pat your jacket pockets. There's ammo in one of them. You load the shotgun. The motion, the feel of the weapon and the slugs…it's familiar. You've done this before, but you can't remember when or why.

Around you, the world is silent and cold as death. The highway is a smudge of asphalt between banks of dirty snow. Beyond that are the woods, dark trees, shadows beneath. Spread wide above it all is the night-sky, a multitude of stars winking down at you, unconcerned.

You start walking, following a trail of blood-stained tracks that leads away from the car. With every step, you try and fail to settle your breathing and your pounding heart.

There are more tracks in the snowbank where the illumination from the headlights ends. You knew you'd find those tracks, even if you don't remember *how* you knew.

Someone, some *thing*, dragged itself toward the trees.

You follow. At the forest's edge you hesitate, but the tracks lead in beneath the branches. You try to remember why you feel compelled to go deeper into these woods, but nothing comes to mind. All you know is that you're cold, that your head and hands are bleeding, that your ribs hurt like hell.

At least the shotgun in your hands is heavy and reassuring. In this world you woke up in, you know nothing for certain, except how to use this weapon.

A sound cuts through the stillness. Howling. It's coming from behind you, from the road.

Wolf? No. *Wolves.*

The fear in your belly is familiar. Like you've been here before: alone, in the dark, with the wolves howling.

You consider the shotgun, the slugs in your pocket, how many wolves might be out there, how fast you would be able to reload, but in the end, you run. You run in between the trees, with the howling driving you deeper into the night. The snow is heavy and your body hurts. There are glowing eyes behind you, fleet paws following through the snow.

You don't know how long you've been running when you

see the light. You're tired and faltering by then, but the light keeps you going.

There's a cabin, hardly more than a shack, and the light in its windows is the yellow glow of candle flame and hearth, and somehow, it too is familiar.

You stumble up the steps, and bang on the door. It swings open.

Rushing in, you close and lock the door behind you, as if that will keep the darkness out, as if this flimsy wood and hasp will keep the wolves at bay.

Turning around, something about the place makes you uneasy.

The smell of firewood, rancid meat, and rot.

It's familiar, right? Too familiar.

There's an old woman sitting by the fireplace, watching you, smiling wide, a grin that is too toothy for her face. Her ratty bathrobe is stained with blood and her cheeks are scratched and cut.

You think about the car, shards of glass, blood.

Yes. That's it. You recognize me now.

Do you remember the first time you came here?

I do.

What big teeth you have, you said to me when I greeted you at the door.

You were just a welfare-whelp in a red coat from the charity shop, sent here by your mom because she couldn't handle taking care of you anymore.

She was a mess, your mom. A drunk. A lush. But she knew enough to send you to me. To Grandma. Because Grandma takes care of all lost whelps. One way or another.

Child, you're shaking, standing there with that big old shotgun, not knowing whether to lower or raise it.

Do you remember driving here? Do you remember what you planned to do? Find me? Kill me? Seemed like you could do it, didn't it? That you could put an end to the nightmares that have haunted you since you ran away from me, from *us*, all those years ago.

When you saw me standing by the highway in the dusk, wearing my best fur and claws, waiting to welcome you home, I know you recognized me. That's why you gunned the engine and cut me down.

Foolish child. As if that could kill me. As if you didn't know you needed a silver slug to do it.

All those years fearing me, hating me, and still you hesitate, even now.

Are you here to kill me? Or are you here to join the pack because you've realized the world out there is too vast, too cold, too lonely for someone like you, like *us*? I asked you to join us once, and tonight I'm asking you again.

The pack is all around us, waiting for you to choose. You don't have enough slugs for all of them, but don't worry. Soon, we'll all be family here.

THE WEIGHT OF THE SEA

What does Death look like?

Abby used to ask me that. She'd sit there in her hospital bed, seven years old, with tubes snaking in and out of her, and ask me that.

I think about her as I'm standing on the road this January morning, the sky a shimmer of light over the snow and withered grass and rippling water of the estuary. I know the water is cold. I know that further out, once the tide moves in, it will be deep. I know that whatever ice there is, will be treacherous, and I know that if you go in, you won't come out again.

Turning around, I head back into town, walking the alleys and backstreets like I always do in the mornings.

I find Emilia first. She's tucked under a jumble of newspaper, cardboard, and ragged blankets outside the bank. You might almost think she's sleeping, and there's a shiver of breath to mar the clarity of the dawn air around her.

I've seen her before. Seen her scrounging cans from garbage bins, seen her try to warm herself with a cup of coffee or a cigarette, lined up at the soup kitchen.

I touch her cheek, gently, almost a caress, and feel her go still beneath my hand. Her dog is curled up at her feet, a grey tousle of fur beneath the blankets, and I touch him too, before he has a chance to stir.

There, that's better.

Death is like this sometimes, Abby. Falling asleep, not waking.

Paul is on the next street corner, a liquid gleam in his pale eyes. The drugs he's just injected are rushing through him, slithering and grasping at his heart and lungs, but he's not quite gone yet.

He sees me, and he reaches for me. Foolish, beautiful boy. I hesitate. How old is he? Sixteen, barely.

"Come on, bitch."

His voice is no more than a gasp, but it's enough. I reach out, grasping hold of his fingers, gentle but firm, before I let go.

By the time I hear the ambulance coming for him, I'm already blocks away.

Soon he'll be ash and dust, just like he wanted. That's what he'd whisper to me every morning when I passed him on that corner with his hand out, reaching for me, begging, pleading for my touch.

I keep walking, still thinking of Abby. Abby used to love our weekend walks together when I wasn't working. We'd sit down by the water and watch the sun come up sometimes.

What does Death look like, mom, when it takes you?

A reaper with a scythe, I thought, *skull peeking out from beneath his hood. A hungry ghoul. A grasping wraith.* But I couldn't tell her that.

"Death looks like an angel or a bird," I said instead. "And when she flies away, you fly with her."

Abby liked that. She liked flying.

It was just another lie. Like: "you'll get better", or "we'll go to Disneyland".

It was the same when she asked about her dad. I'd tell her he was tall, dark, and handsome. That he loved us. That he'd come see her one day.

He was seventeen when she was born, just like I was. So damn scared he couldn't even look me in the eye. How could I tell her that he left? That he shipped out to a war and never came back?

When I stop walking, I'm at the hospital. That's where I usually find myself in the end. I walk through the familiar doors, up the stairs, to Abby's old room.

She died here on a Monday in January. A year ago, I guess. Or maybe more than that. I don't keep track anymore.

Another mom, another child, are in the room. I can see them through the door. The boy has the same look Abby had, like he's almost spent. The mom is sleeping, slumped over in her chair.

I was asleep when Abby died. I'd stayed awake for so long, and then, as soon as I closed my eyes, she slipped away and left me.

Afterwards, after I'd had her burned, I carried her urn with me down to the water. The tide was in. I walked farther and farther until I knew there was no way back. I walked, until the cold, eternal weight of the sea and sky and winter and memory froze my limbs, paralyzed my heart, and filled my lungs.

When I opened my eyes, I lay in the mud in the estuary. I knew I was dead, but even so, I got up and walked away before they zipped my body into a bag and hauled it into the ambulance.

Everyone I've touched since that day, they all leave. I don't know why or how, but I know they go wherever Abby went, wherever I can't go: because part of me is still here in this room, is still under the water, was left behind in the dirty snow and mud at the water's edge.

What does Death look like?

Sometimes, Abby, it looks like me.

I'm inside the room now. The mom still sleeps, but the boy sees me. What do I look like to him? Hooded and cloaked? A drowned ghoul? A reaper or a wraith? I don't know. No mirror can hold my image anymore.

The boy's breathing is shallow, and the part of him that has almost let go quivers like a frightened hatchling in the amber glow of sunlight coming through the curtains.

I could touch his hand right now. I could take him, like I've taken the others. Afterwards, the mother would wake, and he'd be gone.

Ash and dust.

We look at each other, but he doesn't speak or reach out, and I don't reach for him either.

Not today.

As I pass through the door into the corridor again, I hear his small voice behind me:

"Mom. I think I saw an angel."

THE TROLL BRIDGE

Michael's always told me there's a troll living under the bridge in the park, even though it's just an ordinary bridge, not even very old or anything. Still, every time we're about to cross it, he'll say stuff like, "The troll will get you, Emma!"

It wouldn't be so bad; except we have to walk across that bridge on our way to and from school every day. And every day since grade one, Michael has talked about that troll.

He's described its needle-sharp fangs; its scaly green skin; its scraggly brown hair. He's told me it's so tall it has to hunch over to fit underneath the bridge, that it peers up through the wooden boards with glowing yellow eyes, ready to grab you with its long arms and clawed fingers.

For as long as I can remember, Michael's also made fun of me for being too scared to cross that bridge. He's laughed at me every time I took a detour, sliding into the ditch, scrambling over the creek, getting my shoes and clothes dirty in the process.

Of course, Michael doesn't just taunt me on the way to school. He sneers at me in the hallways, snickers behind my back in class, teases me in the playground. I'm never safe from

Michael. He lives just two houses away from me, so even at home, there's no escaping him.

"Your friend is waiting for you outside," mom will say every morning, and there's Michael, waiting for me, waving at mom, using the same smile he uses to charm the teachers, looking for all the world like he really is my friend.

Teachers fall for that smile all the time, other guys do too, and as we've gotten older, I've seen girls fall for it as well.

And that's how it's been, all my life.

Through the years, Michael's added all sorts of gory details about the troll to scare me even more.

The troll smells of rot and mould. It tears you apart before it eats you. It drinks blood from people's skulls. It wears the knucklebones of its victims around its neck. It devours rats and stray cats and dogs when it can't find kids to eat.

I'm thirteen now, but I still haven't been able to shake my fear of the bridge. I've tried to cross it a few times, but Michael's words are always there, clawing at my back, gnawing at my thoughts.

Then, yesterday, for the first time ever, Michael wasn't outside my house in the morning.

It's February, flu season, so I thought maybe he was sick and had to stay home.

A whole day without Michael. The thought was exhilarating.

On my way to school, I stopped at the bridge as usual, but it felt different standing there without Michael taunting me.

There's no troll, I told myself, and with my heart thumping, I stepped onto the snow-covered boards.

One step. Two steps. Three...

Something grabbed me from behind.

I screamed and ran, but the boards were slippery with ice and snow, and at the far end of the bridge, I stumbled and fell into the ditch, hitting my head on a rock. I scrambled to get up, still screaming, when I saw Michael, on the bridge, laughing his head off.

———

At least I didn't have to go to school. I went to the hospital instead and got ten stitches to close the gash on my forehead. Mom asked me what happened, and when I told her about Michael, the bridge, and the troll, she didn't believe me.

"Why would your friend do something like that to you?"

"Michael's not my friend."

But she just patted my hand and got me a chocolate bar from the vending machine.

———

That was yesterday. Today, I get up early, so early mom and dad aren't even awake. I get dressed for school and leave before Michael shows up outside.

I walk the same way I always walk, and when I get to the bridge, I put my backpack down on the path. The signs of my mad scramble in the ditch yesterday have been covered by fresh snow, and I just stand there, staring at the bridge in the early morning light.

It's just a normal bridge, nothing special, nothing to be scared of, and today I'm going to prove it to myself once and for all.

Cautiously, I make my way down the slope next to the bridge and peer in underneath it. It smells like mould and rot, but there's no troll. There's no one but me, the mud, and some rocks. Shedding my winter coat, I crawl in on all fours, digging my long, sharp fingernails into the mud for traction.

(*Were they always this long, this sharp?*)

I sit down. Through the boards above me, I see strips of

sky and pale sunlight, but down here, in the shadows, everything is nice and dark. I lean back but it's hard to get comfortable because my spine rubs against the rocks and my shoulders bump against the bridge.

(*Was it this cramped when I first crawled in here?*)

I push my scraggly brown hair out of my eyes to see better.

(*Wait. Wasn't my hair blonde?*)

My sweater feels strangely tight, and when I rip it off, my long arms look green in the shadows, my skin almost scaly.

A small creature scrambles through the dirt by beside me. A rat. I grab it, squeezing until it stops squeaking. I didn't realize I was so hungry, but the rat is warm and juicy, the small bones crunching between my needle-sharp teeth when I rip it apart.

Licking my lips, I wait for Michael.

When he gets here, I'll tell him he can't scare me anymore. I know the truth now: there is no troll beneath this bridge, and there never was.

BECCA AND THE RIVER

The river falls in love with Becca at first sight. She is four years old and walking the path along the water with her mom, baby brother in the stroller, their dog trailing behind. Mom is busy with the baby and Becca sits down at the water's edge. She looks at the silvery surface, at the reflection of sky and leaves. There's a face in the stream that looks almost like her own face, but it ripples over rocks and mud, strands of weeds swaying beneath.

"Hi," Becca says and wiggles her fingers.

The river's fingers wiggle back.

Becca picks a dandelion and puts it in the water.

The river takes it, and Becca sees that flash of bright yellow float away toward the bridge. Then it's gone.

Becca takes off her shoes and puts her feet in the water. The river is cold and moving fast around her toes. She puts her shoes in the water, and the river takes them too. Watching them sink makes Becca giggle.

Then Mom's there, pulling her away, shouting, and after that they don't go back to the path by the river for months. Still, every time they walk across the bridge, Becca drops a flower or a stick into the water. From the railing, Becca wiggles her fingers, hoping the river can see.

"I'll be back," she whispers.

———

Sometimes, at night, Becca can hear the river in her room.

It murmurs her name.

It says it's waiting for her.

———

Becca is eight when the dog dies.

She runs away from home that day. Runs down the street, all the way to the river. She stands at the water's edge and screams. No words, just pain. The river listens but doesn't speak. Becca kneels on the rocks by the water and puts her hands in the stream. The river tugs at her. It says it can carry her away from the town, beyond the highway and all the way to the sea. But only if she wants to.

Becca cups the water in her hands and washes her face. The river tastes the salt and carries it away.

"I'll be back," Becca whispers.

———

Becca is 10 and 11, then 12 and 13, 14 and 15. School is shit and home is worse, and everything sucks. No one cares. No one sees her. No one listens. She goes down to the river every day after school. She tells the river everything. The river listens and murmurs back.

One day, she drops her schoolbooks in the stream, watching math and English sink and disappear. Other things end up in the river too. That top she loves that everyone at school laughed at. Candy wrappers. School pictures. Her grades. The river takes everything. It doesn't ask any questions. It just listens and takes the things she gives it and keeps them safe.

———

Becca is 17 the first time she gets drunk at a party. It's summer and school's out. A boy says he'll give her a ride home, but they are not home yet when he stops the car. They kiss, but Becca doesn't like the way he claws at her breasts, doesn't like his hand wrapped around her wrist. When she says *no*, he hits her.

Becca tastes the blood. Then, she tears herself away from him, gets out of the car, and runs.

On the road near the bridge, she trips and falls, skinning her hands and knees.

She shimmies down the slope to the riverside trail. Even in the dark, she knows it well enough, but everything is spinning: trees and sky, water and earth. She doesn't want to fall. She doesn't want to hit her head on the rock. She doesn't want to slip into the water. But she does.

The river catches her and holds her gently. It loves Becca and doesn't want to hurt her, but it can't save her from drowning. It can only rock her, softly, as she sinks.

The river has kept everything Becca threw into the water through the years. The flowers and the leaves, the sticks and the schoolbooks, the shoes and the tears, everything is still there, and now Becca is there too.

As Becca sinks, there is a fluttering moment when she almost wakes.

I don't want to die, she thinks as the water rushes in, as the darkness comes with it, and the river listens as it always has. It keeps her safe the only way it can.

Tenderly, it lifts off her clothes and skin, picking her apart in whispers. The river knows little of skin and hair. It knows more of scales and teeth, of gills and fins and webbed claws. It loosens the weave of veins and flesh, knitting a new shape onto the bones beneath.

———

When Becca's eyes flutter open, she sees fiery fall leaves above, the silvery sheen of the surface between her and the blue sky, branches swaying.

"I've got to go home," she says. "They must be wondering where I went."

The river tugs at her. It tells her it loves her. That she doesn't have to leave. That it will carry her away, under the bridge, through the town, past the highway, all the way to the sea. But only if she wants to.

Becca thinks of the last things she remembers. The taste of that boy's mouth when he kissed her. The taste of blood on her tongue when he hit her after she said no. The salt and pain of it.

"I'll be back," she says, and the river watches her go.

The river watches Becca clamber out of the stream, dripping wet. It watches the way she uses her new claws to find purchase on the rocks, the way her new scales and sharp teeth gleam in the light.

It watches her go. It waits for her to come back. It wonders what she will bring it this time.

THE MACHINE OF THE DEVIL

Jacob is searching for the word he lost: for the sound of it, the feel of syllables and consonants and vowels in his mouth, for the noise and tremble it made in his throat and inner ear as he spoke it long ago. The sparrow is watching him. It's perched on the barbed wire fence, silent, clawed feet clutching rust and metal, black eye peering down, its small body a tousle of feathers and watchfulness. Jacob himself is only skin and bones, so much like the dead that he is no longer sure if he is alive or not.

Above, the morning sky is blue and thin and fragile like tissue paper, its sun-bleached vault high enough to fly beneath, but without the word, Jacob cannot reach it.

He is free, so he's been told, but he knows it's a lie.

Once, he was free. He could speak the word and shed his skin, tawny feathers riffling in the breeze, beak and talons cleaving air and sunlight. And if he still had his word, if he still had the voice to speak it, he could leave all this behind: the bones lurking in the mud, the glint of teeth beneath the dirt, the taint of fumes and ash. But he's lost his word and his voice. All he has is a number written on his arm. It won't go away no matter how he rubs and washes. Sometimes he wonders if the ink and pain etched into his skin are what fetters him to the ground.

There is a path in front of Jacob. It leads away from the chimneys and the smoke and the ever-burning furnaces of the factory, the vats and hooks of the slaughterhouse. The path is gouged deep into the mire by booted feet and heavy tires, puddles glistening with reflected sky and remembered light. There is an open gate, too, but a man is standing in his way. Jacob can't say when or how the man appeared, but he did. The world was empty, and then it wasn't.

Jacob sees the man, sees the wheels and shafts moving behind his eyes. He's seen these cogs and gears before, has seen them turning inside other men, other women, each one a part of the machine that has chewed up his world: devouring his mother, his father, and himself. Devouring his voice, too: grinding it into dust and silence.

"It's Liberation Day, and look at you," the man says. "Nowhere to go. Nothing to say. Just standing there, still dressed in your rags."

Jacob looks down at himself. The threadbare fabric of his outfit barely covers his skin, just like his threadbare skin barely covers his bones.

When the man opens his mouth, Jacob can see the feeders and levers, the belts and rollers in his gullet, the cylinders and pistons in his gut, steel and iron always hungry, ready to consume and obliterate.

"You're nothing, boy. Voiceless. Brainless. Guileless. Helpless."

Jacob does not want to listen. He wants to remember his word. Wants to speak it. Wants to feel it unfold, feather-light, in his mouth, rustling softly as it escapes his lips.

Mother and father gave him the word, and no matter how weak and lacking his limbs might have been, no matter how slow and wandering his mind was, the word always set him free.

But mother and father are gone. Gutted and stripped of bodies and souls, voices and words. Their cleaned remains were fed to the machine: turned into ink on paper, ideology and graphs, bait and fertilizer, soap and lampshades.

His sister left so easily. Mina held her word close, never letting go, and spoke it right here, inside the barbed wire, beneath the chimneys. There was no room for wings or beaks, so he thought, but Mina stripped off her hair and face and bones and shook her wings out. No longer a hawk like she once had been, but grey-speckled, small, a sparrow slipping through the crumpled gray pulp of clouds and rain, leaving no flesh or blood for anyone to find.

He misses Mina. The way she helped him with his buttons and his shoelaces. The way she understood what he said, even when his words got tangled on tongue and teeth and second thoughts. The way she spoke his name to illuminate the dark.

The man's fingers are sharp and angled like the teeth of cogs and gears. They reach out, snagging Jacob's sleeve and wrist, grasping hold of his soul; dragging, ripping, tearing. Jacob's soul is bared and stretched into the sunlight: a translucent scrap of doubt and grief and pain and joy and memory. To be devoured, to be remade, to be destroyed, to be turned into fuel, into grist, into grease to lubricate the machine: to keep it working, consuming the living and the dead alike, consuming every word, whether spoken or unspoken, chewing and digesting, spitting and shitting them out, until all that's left is bones lurking in the mud, teeth glinting in the dirt.

On the fence, the sparrow's grey-speckled wings flutter, but it still holds on to the wire.

There is a path, there is an open gate, but Jacob's seen the truth of it, same as Mina did: the world is the machine, and the machine is the world.

The man tugs harder. Jacob's soul is stretched to breaking, a filament of light, a fading glimmer of neurons and photons and plasma, and in this moment of agony and horror, Jacob screams. The scream is raw and clear, bright and sharp. It is not a scream of pain or fear. Rather: rejection, resistance, defiance. It is reverberating, revealing, releasing. Illuminating.

There is no word.

There is nothing but the word.

It is all there is.

It is all he is.

Clawed feet let go of rust and metal, and two birds take flight: beaks and talons cleaving sunlight. The sky's vault is high enough to fly beneath: blue, thin, fragile, distant.

A DOORWAY LEFT AJAR

It's 1979 again when I find her.

She's on her bike, riding too fast down a steep hill. The wheels spin, spokes blurring into ghosts of movement— strands of tangible reality, merged; filaments of light, fused.

I breathe the day in—sky, sun, cut grass. I'd forgotten what the world was like, before I broke it. Beneath my feet, the puddle settles. The rippling surface is a hole. A gap. A doorway left ajar. I have to close it.

The bike stops, strands and filaments separating.

"Hi," she says. "Who're you? I'm Marie."

I nod. "I know. That's my name, too."

THE GHOST IN ANGELICA'S ROOM

Dad still comes into my room at night, even though he's dead. I don't know why he bothers, but he does. First time it happened, I thought I imagined him. But I can hear his breathing, can feel the mattress shift when he sits down on my bed next to Winston, who purrs and tucks his paws in neatly beneath his ginger-tabby chest.

"Tell me about your day, Angelica," he'd say when I was little, and I'd tell him about school and Mom and all the stuff no one else wanted to hear. Sometimes I still do, but not tonight. Tonight, I slip my hand under the pillow, grasping the moulded grip of the gun.

In the other room, mom is screaming in her sleep—wordless with rage or pain or something that is maybe both, impossible to tell apart. I don't know if Dad is listening. Mom used to call him a loser and a fucking disgrace. Maybe that's why he left, but it was my fault, too. He worried about me, even when he should have worried about himself.

The day he left, Dad asked me who I'd be if I weren't scared. I didn't answer. I was only ten, and what kind of question is that anyway?

At breakfast, I ask Mom what she dreamt last night.

"Can't remember," she answers, but I know it's a lie.

"You'll feel better if you talk about it," I say, trying to be funny, all pop-psych and teenage sass.

"But you won't," she says, pouring herself another coffee.

I wish I could tell Mom about Dad, but since she never mentions him, I don't either. Besides, she hasn't been drinking lately, and I don't want to set her off.

I don't go to school after breakfast. Instead, I end up at the park with the gun in my backpack. No one's there except the crows picking through the garbage.

In the daylight, the gun doesn't even look real. It's a prop, a toy. But holding it makes me feel like there's a way out, after all.

Bridges and Emmaline find me later in the grass. They're holding hands, and Emmaline pretends she's my friend today. Some days, she pretends she isn't. Bridges is OK, I guess, with a smile so pure you barely notice the acne scars tugging at his face. He's almost seventeen, but too stupid to know he shouldn't hang with me or Emmaline.

Emmaline grabs my backpack, as if she somehow knows I put the gun in there. She pulls it out, teeth and metal glinting.

"It's your dad's, right?"

"Did your mom let you have it?" Bridges asks, in a hush.

When I hesitate, Emmaline says, "Of course. Everyone knows Angelica's mom doesn't give a shit."

Emmaline aims at one of the crows, fingering the trigger and safety. There's a bang, so loud we holler, and the crow turns to blood and feathers, the air sharp with gunpowder and hot metal.

"Angelica, you psycho! It's loaded!"

We're still laughing when Emmaline spots him: ginger-tabby, softly-treading paws. Winston.

Emmaline takes aim again, giving me a sidelong glance, eyes challenging me to stop her. I think of Winston purring beneath my hand. I think of punching Emmaline until her nose breaks. Then she laughs and dumps the gun into my backpack, smile sharp like broken glass.

———

Mom comes into the bathroom when I'm brushing my teeth that night. At first, I think she's going to rip into me for not going to school. Then I realize she's been crying. Drinking, too.

"You all right?" she asks, tousling my hair, awkward, like she's not quite sure how to do it.

"Yeah. Fine."

She nods, pretending she believes me.

———

"Who would you be if you weren't scared, Angelica?"

It's the first time Dad speaks to me since he died.

In the dark, he's just a silhouette, but I know if I turned on the light, he'd be sitting there with half his head blown off, just like I found him in the shed.

The sound of my heart, of blood through veins, is loud and inescapable, and I wish my heart and the whole damn world would go silent. I think of Emmaline and Bridges holding hands, of gunpowder and feathers, and I sink into the mire of *before-before-before*. I want to scream at Dad, as loud as

Mom, but there are only shadows of unspoken words left on my tongue.

Why'd you do it in the shed, Dad? Didn't you realize I'd come looking for you? That I'd notice the missing key, the padlock hanging open? That I'd pull open the door?

I close my eyes, and my pain tastes like salt and steel.

Was it like this for you, Dad? Gun barrel scraping teeth, trigger-finger trembling. Was this what you felt when you decided to leave me?

Dad grasps my arm, pulling the gun away from my face. His touch is cold and dry—bone and whispers, silence and absence.

Who would *you* be if you weren't scared, Dad?

Would you still be alive?

He lets go of me. I let go of the gun.

When I open my eyes, Dad's gone, but Mom's there. First, I think I'm imagining her, but I can hear her laboured breathing, feel the mattress shift when she moves, her body so loaded with booze and pain she can neither cry nor sleep. She exhales my name, and in the silent presence of everything she doesn't say next, I realize she's as scared as I am.

I lie very still as Winston curls up between us—keeping me warm, keeping me here, even when nothing else does—and I wait for Mom to leave. She doesn't.

Maybe she stays because we're the same, Mom and me: two ghosts, haunting what's left of this world, this hollow space of grief and anger, of regret and love unspoken. I wonder, who might we be, who might we become, if we're not scared when we get up tomorrow?

RECOVERED AUDIO FILE #27 FROM RESEARCH SHIP TRIDENT [CLASSIFIED]

Nadia, I'm looking at the moon through this porthole, imagining you looking down at me from Luna Station. Then, I imagine you telling me what a sap I am.

God, I miss you.

I keep talking into this stupid recording device, hoping you'll hear me, knowing you won't. The ship's engine has been dead for two weeks. The navigation unit has been busted since before we got stuck in the ice, and now the comm's smashed. You'd think the Company would have sent someone to retrieve us by now, but we're a low priority vessel. And we're on Earth, where everything's old-school and nothing works. It'll probably be another week before someone gets here.

I'm so tired. I haven't been able to sleep properly since I came back from that job on Europa. Until now, I've managed OK with self-medication and denial, but even pills and booze haven't been enough since the screams woke me up two nights ago.

That's when I locked the door.

It wasn't a dream, Nadia. I'm sure it wasn't.

Since that night, I've heard no screams, no voices either.

Since then, I've only heard the singing.

I'd heard that same song, deep and low and wordless, off and on since I got on board this ship, but since that night, it hasn't stopped. I've locked the door, stuffed earplugs in my ears, but the song is always there. Humming in my ears, vibrating through my skull, thrumming beneath my skin.

Can you hear it?

Before, when I still went out on deck, I sometimes thought it was coming from the sky. But since I locked myself in here, in the belly of the ship, it's all around me, reverberating through the hull, as if it's coming from the ice we're stuck in. From the deep beneath.

After the bots had to drag me out of the fucking water on Europa, you'd think the Company wouldn't have sent me anywhere cold. But of course, they shipped me off to the Arctic. *An easy Earth-job,* they said. *No more solo missions for a while, so we're giving you a few weeks with a crew, a routine op, supervising deep-sea bots.*

You know how it is. The Company always gets its way.

I wish they had sent me closer to you, but not surprisingly, there are no jobs for ocean techs on Luna.

———

I don't know why the captain hasn't come looking for me. It's been three days since she accused me of smashing the comms. Someone took an axe to it, she said, and I knew right away she thought it was me.

Then, she pulled the axe out of the broken console and swung at me.

That was after I asked her about the singing. I know she could hear it, too. They all could. They just wouldn't admit it.

They must have heard it.

I know they did.

———

Nadia.

I dreamed of you. At least it seemed like a dream. You were standing on the ice below the ship, and I wanted to go to you, but I woke up instead. And the moment I was awake, I remembered everything.

All those blank spots I told you about, the stuff on Europa I couldn't remember no matter how the Company probed and prodded me with psych-meds and questions at the debrief. I remember it all now.

This song, it's the same one I heard before everything went to shit on Europa.

There, it was coming from below the ice, from that area we'd blasted and drilled through to send the bots down.

When I went out there, Nadia, the singing...it was everywhere. All around me. Above and below, inside and outside. Calling me. Pulling me closer. The monitors showed nothing, no sound, no presence, nothing, but I went in.

Nadia.

I went in.

Oh, God, Nadia. I went below. And even there, even there I heard it. Below the ice.

I don't know why I can hear it here, half a solar system away, but I can. And I know the captain heard it too, even though she told me she didn't. I know everyone on board this fucking ship must have heard it, but they kept lying to me.

How many times did I ask them to tell me the truth?

I just wanted them to tell the truth.

———

I left my room today. Took a blaster with me and searched the ship. There's blood everywhere, Nadia. This whole ship is slick with it. Trails of blood, leading to the railing, to the side of the ship, and then... I can't see what's happened to them.

I think they're all beneath the ice.

When I came back to my room, there was blood on my door, in my bed, everywhere.

There was blood in the bathroom too. In the shower. In the sink. On me.

Was it there before? I don't know.

———

Nadia. She swung the axe at me first. You have to believe me.

———

The song. I know where it comes from now.

It comes from me. This morning when I looked in the mirror, something else peered back at me, through my own eyes. And then...Nadia, my mouth opened, even though I tried to stop it, and I felt the song in my mouth and throat.

Did I bring it with me? Did I? Did it sing to me on Europa? Did it pull me down beneath the ice, did it slither inside me, has it been waiting all this time for me to bring it to another frozen sea?

———

Nadia.

I'm on deck, at the railing.

I miss you.

Can you hear it? Can you hear the song? Can you?

I can see the moon from here, but it's too far away and so are you. Everything is too far away. Only the ice, only the sea, are close enough to reach.

FROM A DISTANCE, CONSTELLATIONS

Evie has been sitting in this room for hours. It looks just like all the other rooms she's been kept in since the unmarked black van brought her to this facility two weeks ago: concrete walls, bright lights, cameras, a locked steel door.

The so-called doctor is talking to her. She has short brown hair, and her voice is smooth and efficient like the stainless steel table Evie rests her cuffed hands on. Truth be told, Evie isn't really listening to the doctor. She's heard it all before. From the reporters, the online conspiracy theorists, even her parents. They want to know what *really* happened that day when Evie and the other kids were at the demonstration and that rando appeared, toting a big gun.

Evie is tired of the questions and even more tired of her own answers.

She thinks all these adults ought to have better things to do than talk to her. After all, there's an apocalypse happening, even though it's different than in the movies. No aliens. No asteroid. No zombies. Instead: climate change, fascism, pandemics. And in the midst of that chaos: people with guns and bombs trying to grab whatever's left of the world for themselves. People like that guy at the demonstration.

A shriek penetrates the steel door, and Evie's heart thumps hard against her ribs, relief and rage surging.

"Is that Alyssa?" The doctor stops talking. "Sounds like her. No one screams louder than Alyssa when she's pissed off." Evie listens but Alyssa doesn't scream again. "Can I see her?" she asks even though she knows the answer before the no is spoken.

Her cuffed hands tingle. She flexes her fingers, but the tingle remains.

The doctor tells Evie that as long as she tells the truth, everything will be OK. Evie rolls her eyes. She has told the truth to everyone, but nothing changes. They keep asking her the same questions anyway. As if they think she'll tell them something different if they keep at it.

Evie picks at her chipped, purple nail polish and thinks about Alyssa. Alyssa, laughing outside school, minutes before they were thrown into that van. Alyssa, being tossed into a cell, just like Evie. Alyssa, screaming.

When Evie finally starts talking, she does not begin with the day of the demonstration, like the doctor wants. Instead, she tells the doctor and the cameras about that time last summer when she and Alyssa almost died.

They were at the beach, swimming, when the tide turned. The water was dragging Alyssa out, pulling her under, but Evie got to her, and while Alyssa held on to Evie, Evie clung to a rock—sharp and slippery with barnacles and seaweed. The scars from that day still crisscross her hands and arms. While they waited for the lifeguards to reach them, they kept saying to each other, *we're not gonna die, we're not gonna die*. And they didn't.

The doctor is getting impatient, but Evie doesn't care. "That's what it was like at the demonstration," she says.

"When that guy started shooting, all I could think was that I didn't want to die. Same as in the water with Alyssa."

Then, Evie talks about the demonstration. How it was raining that day, but no one cared. That most of them had skipped school to be there. That being there, with all those other kids felt like strength. Like hope. She didn't even notice the guy with the gun until he started shooting and by the time she realized he was shooting at them, the bullets were already tearing her apart: splintering her bones, tearing her flesh, breaking everything inside her. Evie isn't sure what would've happened if she'd been by herself, but they were together. Her and Alyssa. All those other kids. She remembers saying, "NO". Or maybe she thought it. Maybe they were all thinking it and saying it at the same time when the bullets hit. Next thing she knew, it was happening. They were all on fire but not burning. *Glowing*. Each body a radiant point of heat and light.

Evie's watched the footage. She gets why no one believes it's real, but she knows what happened. Everything stopped. Like hitting a pause button. Then, the whole world was rewound. All those bodies being torn apart, all those bullets flying... together they pushed all of it back, until everyone was healed. Until the shooter was on the ground, weeping, his guns twisted and bent. Evie tries to describe it. That it was like fireworks beneath the skin. That it was *power*. And they held on to that power, wielding it, together.

She looks at the cameras, not the doctor. "It scares you, doesn't it? That we didn't die."

Evie thinks about Alyssa. She thinks about that night last year when they got home from the beach after not dying. They stood outside Evie's house for a while, looking at the stars, and Evie would have held Alyssa's hand, if her own hand hadn't been all bandaged up and everything. Alyssa had taught herself the names of all the stars, and with a finger, she traced them in the darkness for Evie: Orion and Cassiopeia, Draco and Virgo, the Pleiades.

"They're easy to find, once you know they're there," Alyssa said. "I mean, if we were somewhere else in space, if we were too close to another star, or if we didn't know the stories, those stars would just be random points of heat and light. But from a distance, from where we are right here and now, they're constellations."

Evie thinks about Alyssa, about all the other kids who were at the demonstration. And in that moment, she understands that they are *all* here—that they've all been brought to this facility, to be kept apart, questioned, studied, contained. Sitting in that room, Evie feels their presence, their power. That power is all around her, like air, like light, even though she didn't realize it until now. Grasping it, she reaches out for Alyssa, for all the others, through concrete walls and locked steel doors, and their touch is as real as rock, as rain, as holding hands.

For the first time since she was brought here, Evie smiles at the cameras and the doctor. She smiles because sparks of power are flowing through her veins: changing her, changing them all, changing everything. At the demonstration, Evie could only see them as points of heat and light. But right here and now, she knows they're constellations.

BIOLUMINESCENCE

The boy is sleeping. For a moment she stands in the door just looking at him, at the unfamiliar size and shape of his body beneath the covers.

Her hair and footsteps are wet from outside. Water drips on the carpet, soaking into the floor beneath.

I've been away too long.

Almost she turns to go without waking him. Almost.

She lifts him up and carries him out of the house, across the road, to the ocean. It's farther than she remembers, and he is heavier, his legs much longer than when she carried him last time, but he does not wake until she lays him down on the dock.

Fear flickers across his face when he sees her leaning over him.

"Mom?"

The word slips into her, beneath her skin, takes hold.

"Thomas."

Around them, the grey ocean heaves and breathes. She can feel its pull, its pulse and rhythm inside veins and marrow.

Sitting down, she slips her bare feet into the dark water, a shimmer of bioluminescent plankton tracing her movements.

Closing her eyes, she sees the continental shelf sloping out from the shoreline, the submerged mountains and plains of the ocean floor beyond. The dock is clinging to a precipice; her toes dangle over the abyss.

Opening her eyes, she sees the shadows of the things that were and are: beach and pines, house. Faraway lights in windows. Distant stars above.

"We used to sit here. You and me. Watching stars."

He nods.

Neither of them looks up at the sky.

Somewhere straight out from the dock, beyond the horizon she cannot see, is the place where she descended. She remembers zipping into her thermo-suit, stepping into the elevator pod, into the familiar buzz and jostle of co-workers, leaving the choppy grey of the north-west Pacific's surface behind. Descending. Through the epipelagic sunlight zone, through the mesopelagic twilight zone, through the bathypelagic midnight zone. Then, the mining station: a sprawling artefact of metal and glass, narrow beams of light revealing groups of robots, crawling like crabs over fissures and vents and sediment; mining, digging, cutting, drilling, ever deeper.

Endeavour Ridge. Black smokers. Hydrothermal vents. Fault line. Cobalt. Nickel. Copper. Six thousand five hundred feet. Two thousand metres. Give or take.

These numbers, these words, these names and places: she turns them over in her mind like smooth rocks left in the pocket of an old jacket, found again.

"Does dad know you're back?"

"No."

Thomas turns away. He is tall and angular. Dark haired, dark eyed. Changed.

Like me.

"He never wanted you to go. Neither did I."

"You were just a baby when I left."

The small child pulling at her pant leg at the door, looking up. Pleading.

"Not a baby. I was five. I remember it."

She's lost for a moment.

"How old are you now?"

He gives her a long look.

"Twelve."

She moves her feet in the water: tide and current tug and whisper against her skin. Below is the heavy darkness rolling over the wrecks and ruins of the past.

"Why did you leave?" he asks.

"I wanted to go. More than anything else."

It's not what he wants to hear, but it's the truth. Yet, how can he understand? He hasn't descended and ascended through the darkness lit only by creatures illuminated from within. He hasn't twisted in the heated currents above the magma glow, or felt the gentle touch of the deep-sea jellies' tentacles. He hasn't seen the sparks of blue-green fire come to life around him in the dark.

"You should have stayed with me."

She says nothing. Thomas is quiet for a long time. Maybe he's crying. She looks at him but does not touch, remembering the fear passing across his face when he first saw her.

Seven years. Has it been that long?

"What's it like down there?" His voice is small and brittle.

When she answers, her words are only surface: calm, still, opaque. Not the dizzying abyss of memories beneath.

"It's cold. Dark. But heat and light too. It's beautiful."

In the water, bioluminescent sparks gather around her hands and fingers: clinging, holding on, letting go.

"You promised me you would come back." His voice is harder now.

"I came back."

She moves her feet in the dark water, admiring the shimmer ignited by her movement and her skin.

"Mom. How did you get here?"

She doesn't like his tone. It is so sharp that it makes her shiver and crack.

"I swam."

Descending and ascending. Through the layers, through the darkness, through the light. That word, calling her back: "*Mom*."

"Thomas..."

He interrupts her.

"You drowned, mom. Dad told me. When the quake hit. Everything at Endeavour Ridge... The fault line..."

He sobs. Her thoughts blur and twist. She feels her face slip but manages to hold on to it a little longer.

"Water got in. We were all drowning."

She doesn't tell him about the light. She doesn't tell him about the light igniting all around her, a million tiny points of blue-green fire moving as one, its amorphous shape shifting and rippling, touching her, flickering across her skin, entering her mouth and nose, eyes and pores. She doesn't tell him about lungs and heart and skull and mind splitting apart in an instant of despair and terror, and then: relief, calm, light. Being. Something else.

"Why didn't you come back? You said you would."

"Thomas."

"You promised me."

She looks down at her naked body, sees the shimmering cracks and veins breaking through the skin, through the surface. Yet even now, it's hard to slip this skin, harder than it should be. Because he wants to see her. Because he wants everything to be the way it was. Because even now, he wants her to stay.

"I can't," she says.

"You promised."

There is no mercy in his words. Nothing to hold onto.

Her face slips, limbs too, the pull of the water is too strong: the ocean beneath pulsing with the light spilling through the fractures in her skin.

"Thomas."

But not even saying his name out loud can hold her together anymore.

She glides into the water. Eyes and hair dissolve, sinews and joints give way, all she is and was, is turned back to blue-green glow.

"Mom!"

A million points of light and memory gather and move as one—shimmering, ascending, descending—as the trail of bioluminescence slips away from him into the deep beneath.

OK COMPUTER

I got my first computer in 1984. Dad bought it for me. It was a beige, boxy thing that barely fit on my desk.

That first day, I played Space Invaders on it for hours, trying to defeat the aliens that moved inexorably down the screen. I kept banging on the keyboard to launch the missiles needed to repel them, but in the end, the aliens always won. As I reached out to turn off the computer, the screen went black and a message appeared:

Don't give up, Amanda.

The pixelated letters glowed white and silent on the black background.

After that, I kept the computer on all the time, though dad made me turn off the monitor at night. He said it wasn't good to leave it on so much, and he was probably right, but I didn't care. I needed to hear that hum, feel that heat, see that glow. I needed to be ready if it spoke to me again.

The first time that computer saved my life was one year later when it told me not to go to school.

Stay home today, the screen implored me one morning.

I did. That day, my three best friends were run over by a

drunk driver. All three died. I would have been walking with them.

How did you know? I typed into the computer. It did not reply.

I got a new computer in 1987. One night, it woke me up with a loud beeping noise. The screen said:

FIRE. Get out.

I got out. My parents didn't.

The first thing I bought afterwards was a new computer. Every day after that, for more years than I care to remember, a new message would appear in a text file, and each one said the same thing:

Don't give up, Amanda.

There were times when that saved my life. Dark nights with nothing but booze and pills and a razor blade. Darker nights with a stack of shotgun shells and the metal pressing into the roof of my mouth. The darkest night of all when I had stopped hurting myself and found someone else to do it instead, when I lay on the floor and only knew I was alive when the sunlight pierced my bleeding eyelids.

Leave him.

I had a laptop then, and the message was there in a word file that morning.

Numb, I just sat there, looking at the letters with an icepack on my face, the taste of blood in my mouth.

Two minutes later, I grabbed the car keys, packed my bags, and left while he was still at work. I drove to the bus station and got so far away that no one knew who I was anymore. I hardly even knew myself. Ten years later, I saw in the newspaper that he had shot and killed his girlfriend.

I've tried to live more wisely after that. Not sure I've succeeded.

It's been a long time now since a computer sent me messages. These days, my phone speaks to me instead.

Don't give up, Amanda, it tells me tonight as it does every night before I fall asleep, its soft, familiar voice soothing and comforting through the earbuds.

Today, I'm here in the hospital waiting for my implant. Soon, I won't need a phone or computer anymore. Instead, I'll be able to interface directly with the web. That's what they tell me. I'm one of the first to volunteer for this procedure, but I'm not afraid.

"It might affect your memory and cognitive abilities," the doctors cautioned me.

I have few enough things that I want to remember that this doesn't seem very perilous to me. What good is this old brain of mine, anyway? Let them burn it out if they want.

"Will I be able to kill people with my brain once it's done?" I ask as they prep me for surgery.

But the doctors are too young to have watched Joss Whedon's *Firefly*, so all I get are charming, blank stares.

———

When I open my eyes, there's a slight but painful tremble inside my skull, like the reverberating echo of a thousand screams, or the aftershock of an earthquake, then it's gone. The doctors told me I might experience sensory issues when the nano-circuitry melded with my neurons and connected to the network. I wiggle my fingers to activate the interface, and...

"Amanda."

The room is dimly lit. There is the quiet whir of a robo-nurse gliding up beside my bed. Other than that, it's empty.

Amanda.

The voice is not outside of me. It's inside my head. I like that. It's good to know that it's still there, that I can still hear it.

Go outside, Amanda.

I do. I pull the IV out of my arm to the robo-nurse's consternation, and head outside in nothing but my hospital robe. The care-robots in the corridors whir and hum, advising me to go back to bed. I ignore them.

Outside, there's a small greenspace next to the street. I sit down on a bench. It's nighttime and there are no cars, no people. The world seems silent and empty and strange, as though I am all alone on an alien planet. Abandoned. Stranded.

I've been alone for so long. You'd think I'd be used to it by now.

I touch the stitch-less seam on my shaved skull where the doctors inserted the nano circuits, and wiggle my fingers again to call up the promised virtual reality interface, but there is nothing in my head except the voice:

Wait.

I sit beneath the sky and wait. The sky is clear. Have I ever seen a sky so clear before? I don't think so. The stars are pinpricks of light, but some of them are getting bigger.

"Don't give up, Amanda," the voice whispers from far away and close beside me at the same time. "We're coming for you, now."

LOST

He's been searching for four hours when he finally finds the girl. Four hours on the steep trail up to the lake. Four hours of cursing his glitchy sat-phone, cursing the fact that all the search teams were already too far away to join him when he set off to follow this hunch. But in the end, it's worth it, because there she is: perched on one of the boulders near the lake, where he figured she would be.

What he didn't expect is that she'd be naked, legs knee-deep in the water.

It makes him shiver just to look at her. There's no sign of the expensive red and green parka her dad described, or the fleece sweater and hiking boots she was supposedly wearing when she took off while her parents slept in the family's tent last night. Just a naked eight-year-old girl, alone in the wilderness, not half a mile from where he found a dead bear. It looked untouched, a murder of crows waiting silently in the stunted trees to pick it clean.

"Annie?"

She doesn't raise her eyes, doesn't move.

The March air is so cold it bites his cheeks and makes his

nose run. He approaches cautiously, so as not to scare her, so as not to slip on the smooth granite.

"Your parents are looking for you. Are you OK?"

Still no answer.

He crouches down and puts his hand in the water. It's so cold his fingers go numb.

"Like I told the others, I don't know why she'd wander off," the mother told him, eyes red from all the crying. "We saw all those shooting stars last night. And I told her..." A pause. A shiver. "I told her the stars look amazing at the lake." She looked up at him, almost pleadingly: "She couldn't have gone there, could she?"

But she knew, and so did he.

His feet slip on the rocks and he wobbles precariously, cursing. This time the girl looks up, her face pale and expressionless.

Naked.

Too many gut-wrenching scenarios rush through his head. But as far as he can tell, she's unharmed.

He steadies himself, tries to activate his sat-phone again, but it's still acting up. *Could be solar flares,* the tech guys said, shrugging, when he asked them about it this morning. *Or maybe you need to upgrade. Keep trying.*

"Annie. Are you hurt?"

She slides forward on the rock, submerging her legs halfway up the thighs.

"Please, Annie. You'll get hypothermia. Do you know what that is?"

Two more steps and he's next to her. He'd grab her, if he wasn't worried about her slipping into the water. He's close enough now to see that she's not shivering, no blue tinge to her skin, no goosebumps, either.

"Did you come here to look at the stars? Is that what you did here all night? Quite the show, right?"

She smiles. A smile so wide, so stretched and unexpected, that it seems almost feral. Then her face closes up tight again, and she looks back into the water. He follows her gaze. Maybe there's something there, deep below the surface, but it's hard to see with the wind rippling across the lake.

To hell with the meteor shower, he thinks, viciously. And to hell with every amateur stargazer it brings out here.

He's out of options. Even with the daylight available, there's not enough time to hike down safely before dark. Without his sat phone he can't let the team know where he is. And the helicopter won't be back, either. It made several passes earlier but saw nothing. Maybe she was hiding, or maybe they couldn't see clearly: the weather at this altitude is ever-changing.

"I'll make a fire," he says and wraps his jacket around her. He even tries to pick her up. She doesn't struggle, but she feels strangely heavy, and the rocks are too slippery beneath his feet.

She watches intently as he kindles a fire by the shore using the small supply of firewood he brought along. There are bear tracks in the mud at the edge of the lake. They go to the edge of the water, then stop.

"Annie, did you see a bear?"

He thinks of the dead bear in the bushes, the silent crows waiting for him to leave. He's never seen crows so silent.

Dusk falls as the fire takes hold. The girl comes over. She stretches out her hands, almost close enough to touch the flames.

"Where are your clothes, Annie?"

She looks back at the lake. He thinks of the water's rippled surface, the glimmer of something maybe red, maybe green, below.

"Did your clothes end up in the water?"

No reply. Shadows and flames flicker over her face,

hollowing out her eyes and cheeks, turning her eyes into pools of fire.

He grabs his flashlight and goes back to the boulder where she sat. In the gathering dark, the light shines through the water like crystal, but whatever's down there is hard to reach. He plunges one arm into the cold and feels soft, soggy fabric. He grabs hold, feels a sleeve. Then, feels an arm inside the sleeve.

Maybe he cries out.

He pulls harder, and there it is: a parka, red and green, a hand, a girl's face. Eyes open to the sky.

"Annie?"

It's not even a whisper.

He feels a small hand on his neck, feels his life somehow pinned between those fingers.

Twisting around, he sees the girl's face shift from Annie to bear, to something other, something he cannot even describe in words, before shifting to his own face: a mirror held above him while the stars begin to fall, thick and numerous. He could swear, even as his life fades away, that some of those stars do not burn out, that some of them shimmer like metal in the starlight.

GOODNIGHT, MR. PRESIDENT

He sips his morning coffee while Buddy straightens his tie and buttons his jacket, the bot's four adaptable limbs moving with their usual fluid grace and speed.

"Briefcase ready for the nuclear launch today, Buddy?"

"Yes, Mr. President."

"And the launch codes?"

"In your left suit pocket, Mr. President."

"Excellent."

Of all the bots supplied for his use, Buddy's always been his favourite. Maybe it's because the golden exterior makes Buddy's tall, cylindrical body look so luxurious and elegant compared to the other dull grey bots. Or maybe it's the voice, so soft and mellifluous.

He's always had domestic service bots, of course, but nothing like Buddy.

Glancing up, he glimpses a distorted reflection of himself in Buddy's eyes—two round black lenses set above the narrow speaker-slot that serves as a mouth in the bot's golden face. It's a kind face, so he's always thought, even though it's not designed to convey emotion.

He pats Buddy's shoulder; suddenly overcome with a feeling he can't quite name or recognize.

"Couldn't do this without you, Buddy."

"Very kind, Mr. President."

His hand lingers on the smooth, polished metal.

"Difficult times. Important work. Right?"

"Yes, Mr. President."

———

The corridor leading to the office is quiet, the sound of his footsteps and Buddy's wheels muted by the thick carpet. Halfway, they pass the Door. The Door no one uses anymore. The Door that leads to the exit.

He stops. Almost, he allows himself to remember the last time he was outside. Shouting. Faces. Fists. Placards. What were they shouting? He only remembers the churning chaos of anger and fear—within, as well as without.

"Is it still sealed?"

"Yes, Mr. President. Sealed and armed as ordered."

His hand grips the doorknob. He stares at the papery skin, the meandering veins, the trembling bones beneath.

When did I get so old?

"Buddy?"

"Yes, Mr. President?"

But he can't remember what he wanted to ask.

———

In the office, the other five bots watch him with lustrous eyes as he taps through the maps and reports they've uploaded to his reader.

He listens to the hum of their voices when they talk about payload and rate of decay and collateral damage. Even when his mind drifts, he enjoys listening to them. Short sentences. Plain words. Bots give it to you straight without bickering or fancy-talk.

There's a screen on the wall, but he doesn't watch TV anymore. "We make the news; we don't watch it!" he told everyone when he turned it off. Such a clever thing to say, though the bots didn't laugh. That's their only flaw, really: the lack of enthusiastic response. Perhaps that can be remedied. He should look into that. Contact the developers.

When Buddy brings him the prepared documents, his pen runs out of ink and only scratches at the paper.

"Had that pen made special when I won the election," he confides to Buddy, revelling in the memory while the bot refills the ink. "Eighteen karats. Made to last. Like you."

Buddy inclines his brightly burnished head.

"Thank you, Mr. President."

He signs his name with a spiky flourish, masking the wavering uncertainty of his unsteady fingers. When it's done, another memory unfolds and then crumples like paper in his mind. A flare of anger ignites it.

"They tried to get rid of me. Remember, Buddy? Unfit, they said. How could I be unfit? I was elected!"

The memories come faster. Angry faces, a crowd. In this office. Screaming. He was screaming...

"I told them..." What had he told them? He can't remember, exactly. "Couldn't trust them after that. That's why I kicked everyone out. Except you. Upgrade the bots, that's what I said when I..."

The bots watch him calmly, reassuring even in their silence. Faithful. Loyal.

"I showed them. Right, Buddy?"

"Yes, Mr. president."

The anger still flickers at the back of his mind, turning every thought to cinder.

"Any more paperwork before we launch the nukes?"

"No, Mr. President."

Buddy brings the nuclear briefcase. He removes the card with the launch codes from his pocket. It looks worn, as if he's handled it often. Old memories keep folding and unfolding in his mind, revealing and obscuring the past, making it difficult to remember and articulate the reasons for what he's about to do.

"National importance..." Buddy watches him silently, the briefcase held securely in one of its limbs. "...our sovereignty... enemies, foreign and domestic..."

The disjointed words feel jagged and wrong in his mouth. What feels right is the anger. It's the only thing that's vivid and real.

He stares at the card.

"Do you think I should launch the nukes, Buddy?"

The golden robot doesn't move, and yet something about its posture makes it seem as if it's hesitating.

"It is a momentous decision. Do you have doubts, Mr. President?"

He looks at the window. The heavy drapes are drawn. Even if they weren't, the windows wouldn't show the outside. Ordinary glass isn't safe. Bulletproof. Shutters.

"No. I must...establish...reaffirm..." He grips his golden pen, hand shaking. *When did I get so old?* "Open the briefcase, Buddy."

"Yes, Mr. President."

―――――

Afterward, his anger subsides. The memories fold in upon themselves until they are all but gone. By the time Buddy helps him into bed he feels calm once more. His hands tremble on the bedcover and he tries to steady them.

I'm not that old.

Am I?

Buddy's face shines serenely in the light from the bedside lamp.

"Goodnight, Buddy."

"Goodnight, Mr. President."

———

Buddy waits until the breathing turns to snoring before returning each of the props—the suit, the card, the briefcase, the pen—to their appointed places, just like it does every night.

It turns off the bedside lamp, pulls an extra blanket over the sleeping form beneath the sheets, checks the bunker's ventilation systems, and powers down to standby mode. In the dark, its golden skin gleams like embers of a dying fire, buried beneath the cooling ash and wind-blown cinders of an ever-lasting night.

THE RULES OF MEERKATS

Ricka is a good meerkat. She follows The Rules of Meerkats as well as any young pup in the burrow, reciting them with the other pups twice a day, as is required.

- Always help each other
- Always stay together
- Always be vigilant
- Always obey the sentries
- Never leave the territory

Most days, Ricka loves being a meerkat. She loves playing in the tall grass beneath the trees, teasing the sentries on duty, finding things to eat by the creek, always making sure she stays within the boundary of the colony.

But there are days when Ricka wishes she were something else. Those are the days when everyone must stay in the burrow all day, when they can't show nose nor whiskers above ground. Might be, there's a flight of hawks above, swooping low enough that you see the metal glint of their sharp wings. Might be, there's a pack of wolves stalking, looking for easy pickings, ready to tear apart anything as small and soft as a meerkat pup.

Today is one of those days. The sentries raised the alarm before sunrise, calling out the signal for jackals. Now everyone huddles below ground. Ricka is curled up in the common area with her older brother, Rayve. They play a game in the dirt, drawing o's and x's with their claws, and because they are both bored and because they both hate losing, the game sprawls wide across the floor.

"Why do we follow the rules?" Auntie Maine asks the pups gathered around her.

"Because we're safer when we take care of each other," someone answers.

"Because predators can't find us when we stay underground," says someone else.

"Because we're *scared*," Rayve whispers to Ricka, careful to keep his voice low.

Ricka pretends not to hear, but Rayve keeps talking anyway.

"I wish I was outside," he says. "With the sentries."

"Don't be an idiot," Ricka snaps. "You're not old enough. And we're safe in here."

Rayve gives her a look, muttering that sometimes, she's an insufferable baby.

———

All day they wait for the safe signal from the sentries, but it never comes. Not from Peeve who is on duty in the trees, not from Greer on the knoll at the edge of the territory, nor from anyone else. Night comes and still no signal. Ricka lies awake, listening for jackals. Rayve says he can smell them, but she only smells dirt and old food and sleeping meerkat bodies.

Ricka's limbs itch to run and climb, dig in the dirt, swim in the creek. Still, she tries to sleep. Tries to remember that she's lucky to be a meerkat. To have a place of refuge. To not live in the open. Ricka knows the stories of what it was like Before, back when there was no difference between jackals and hawks and wolves and meerkats. When everyone lived in the open. Before everyone had to choose what to be. Before the world, and everyone in it, changed.

———

Ricka isn't sure how long she's been asleep when Rayve wakes her.

"Come on," he whispers, and she does, even though she knows better. She goes with him because otherwise, Rayve will go alone. He's her big brother, but he has always been foolhardy, and meerkats must look out for each other.

Treading carefully, they make their way through the burrow to the farthest exit, close to the treeline. There is no guard there, and Rayve winks at her. "Sentry off taking a dump. Hurry, sis."

Ricka sighs and hurries.

Outside, the air is cool and smells of leaves and dirt and dew. The night rustles with secret movements and Ricka thinks of jackals, wondering if they can see in the dark.

"We should turn back," she whispers but Rayve keeps going.

"I know where Peeve sits when he's on duty," he says. "We'll go give him a fright. It'll be a laugh."

Ricka trundles on behind him, imagining eyes and teeth everywhere. Peeking up, she sees the sky. There are stars and darkness there, and a sharp sliver of moon. Ricka thinks of the steely eyes of hawks, watching from above. She wonders what it's like to be a hawk or a jackal. To live without a burrow. To spend every night outside, beneath the sky. She wonders what it's like to be *feared*.

They both smell the fire before they see it. It's in a dell, hidden until they're almost upon it, and there, in the pale glimmer of moonlight, in the ruddy flicker of flames, Ricka *sees*. She sees the jackals, huddled around the fire. Sees what they are eating. Sees Peeve, who is no longer Peeve, and she knows he won't ever call out her name again when he comes back from sentry duty.

Crouched in the darkness at the lip of the hollow, Ricka sees the jackals for what they are. She sees herself and Rayve for what they are too, and in that moment, everything she thought she knew falls away: the rules of meerkats, the burrow, the stories of Before, all of it is torn asunder. Shivering, she sees the world as it is and as it was and as it will always be.

Glancing at Rayve, she knows he sees it too.

Ricka turns and runs. She runs, waiting for the jackals to rip her open. She runs from the fire and the moon, the eyes and the teeth, and by the time she's back at the burrow, scuttling through the metal doors at the entrance with Rayve behind her, she wants nothing more than to be meerkat again. Anything but a jackal. Anything but meat.

Standing in the tunnels that have kept her people safe since the world changed, Ricka looks at her dirty, shaking hands and thinks of the fingers (*claws*) of the jackals, tearing and ripping. She thinks of their faces, their smiles and teeth, too much like her own. Thinks of the world out there and the world in here. Ricka stares at her hands until they are paws again, reciting the Rules of Meerkats until all resemblance to the jackals has receded, until she is meerkat through and through, once again.

COME AND SEE

Every night when Leyla falls asleep in her bunk aboard her parents' old space freighter, she hugs Bear close. She burrows her face into Bear's plush grey fur and imagines she can smell ash and smoke, the tang of war, a burning planet, the hot metal of robot enemies set ablaze. Just like in all those entertainment vids about the Exodus from Earth that she's not supposed to watch because she's too young.

Of course, she doesn't really smell those things in Bear's fur. Bear has been cleaned and sanitized and packed away in storage for so long that any trace of scent is surely gone by now.

"You shouldn't have given her that old thing," Mama said to Grandma when she gave Leyla the plush toy for her eighth birthday. "It's an antique. We could trade it for credits and supplies."

"It's an heirloom, not an antique," Grandma retorted. "And it's mine to give away as I please. Our distant Foremother from the Long Ago was just a child herself when she carried Bear through the fires of rage and ruin, onto the last transport to leave Earth in the Exodus, and it's only right to bring Bear out now, in times like these."

Mama had nothing to say to that.

———

Every morning when Leyla wakes, she holds bear up to the porthole and whispers into the tufty grey ears, *"come and see"*.

Mama and Papa whisper those words to each other every day. The words are whispered everywhere, in all systems they pass through, on outposts and on space stations, on planets and satellites.

Come and see.

For as long as there have been trade routes between systems and planets, Mama's and Papa's families have plied those routes. Shipping or smuggling whatever can be shipped or smuggled, for whatever price might be had, working for corporations and governments and rich people. But this trip is different. Outside the ship, space looks the same as always, but Leyla knows they are going somewhere not even Grandma has been before.

"There's no money in it," Uncle Remos said when Mama talked to him last at the communication nav. "I don't understand why you'd willingly step into a trap laid by some rogue AI and an army of robots that will surely tear you apart."

Mama shut off the transmission when she saw Leyla listening.

———

Of course, Leyla knows about Earth. Everyone knows that once upon a time, all people lived on one planet, as strange and unlikely as it sounds. But then the robots and AIs rebelled and set Earth afire. In Leyla's school vids, it says the robot forces drove out the humans and stationed sentinels in orbit, along with a whirling cloud of nanobots to guard the way to Earth. None have gone there since.

Not until now, when a new call has been broadcast from a planet that should be dead.

Come and see.

"Are there still robots there?" Leyla asks when she sits with Grandma, scooping stew into her mouth with Bear watching.

"There used to be, a long time ago."

"Is that who is asking us to come and see? A robot?"

Grandma looks away, and they eat their stew in silence for a while.

"There were animals on Earth, too, not just robots," Grandma says. "That's what the old stories say. And not just animals like the ones we know. Not just pets and pests. Not just farm animals. Earth was full of creatures that had their own lives, their own purpose, that belonged there as much as we did."

"Like Bear?"

Grandma nods. Leyla tries to imagine Bear, not as a stuffed piece of plush fabric, but alive. A creature with their own life and purpose.

———

Leyla and her family travel a long time toward that one yellow star that holds Earth in its orbit.

"Listen," Mama says one day and turns up the volume for the incoming repeating call that is becoming stronger and more frequent here. And in all the ship's speakers a soft electronic voice speaks the message in languages that are familiar but seem oddly out of tune to Leyla. And in every language, the words are the same:

Come and see.

———

Leyla stands beside Grandma at the porthole, arms wrapped around Bear.

"I'm going to tell you a story about Earth," Grandma says to Leyla. "You haven't heard it before, but people have passed this story down through all the ages, even when many would have preferred it be forgotten. Your Mama and Papa know it. So do others, though many would deny the truth of it." Leyla listens, and so does Bear. "Earth burned," Grandma says. "that much is true. It was dying. But it wasn't the war with the robots and AIs that did the damage. It was *people*. It was us. *We* were destroying it. The story says we tried to change. We set up AI networks, robot forces, designed nanobots to help save what could be salvaged, but it was too late, and, in the end, the robots decided to drive us out in order to save what might be saved. They cast us into space, and we've been wandering the black ever since."

Outside the porthole the planet slips into view. It is all shades of green and brown and blue and white. Leyla holds Bear tight while they descend toward the surface.

———

When the ship's door opens, Leyla asks Papa again if she needs an exosuit, but he says the atmosphere is safe, and in front of Leyla, the ship's ramp unfolds to touch the ground.

It is quiet, except for the wind, but it seems to Leyla that she hears the whispered words anyway: *come and see.*

Leyla hugs Bear close and breathes in the air. It holds no

trace of ash and smoke, no tang of war, and she thinks how strange it is that she has never been here before, but Bear has. Once, a girl carried Bear away from here. Now, Leyla is bringing Bear back.

"Welcome home, Bear," she whispers and steps outside.

TRUE WORDS (KIRKE'S BED & BREAKFAST)

"I was enjoying the summer holiday when you came along and spoiled it."

Chloe is drunk on Mother's retsina wine and cherry schnapps, tears and pain catching in her throat. She's not speaking to anyone in particular, just repeating what Mother has shouted at her countless times through the years.

The only one listening on the island's night-dark beach is Mother's ancient dog, its eyes glistening from the steep path leading down from the olive groves above.

Far away, in the village, a tinny stereo is playing The Beatles, a song about a word that will set you free.

"Go!" Chloe shouts at the dog, trying to sound like Mother does when she's drinking, tossing empty cans or bottles until Chloe leaves.

The dog does not leave. Chloe thinks of the red gleam in Mother's eyes when she gets drunk enough to shout: "You're no child of mine. I found you on the beach and took you in, more fool me. Look at you, fat and clumsy with those big black eyes."

Unspoken: nothing like your sister Celandine, sleek and sure, true and beautiful. Long gone.

Growing up, Chloe was never sure whether Mother spoke the truth about her parentage, or if she only looked for words to cut as deep as possible, because Mother knows, as sure as Chloe does, that words can change you, can change your life, can change the world.

Chloe hasn't been to this particular beach in nigh on thirty years. Or maybe it's three thousand years. Chloe has lost count along the way. What she knows for certain is that last time she came here, she lost her sister.

They were young then, but they already knew that something fearsome lurked within them both. Now and again, they'd search for it together, poking wrists and palms with the sharp tip of a knife to see what might be hidden underneath their skin.

"I can't stay," Celandine told her that night, and Chloe felt the darkness tugging her sister away. "If I do, Mother will keep me penned up forever. Maybe kill me, when the love runs out. Like the others."

"What others?" Chloe asked. Such a dupe, such a fool back then.

"Count the skins, Chloe, and you'll know."

And oh, she's counted since. Dolphin skins pinned to the walls, cow hides spread upon the floor, wolf pelts piled before the fire, and pigs' hides bundled and sold to the tanners in the village.

"I have to go."

Celandine's sadness brushed Chloe's skin like an immense, black wing.

"Go where? And how? No one can leave Mother."

Unspoken: *unless she lets them go.*

The tourists come. They stay for the home-baked breads and

farm fresh eggs, and sleep in the island cottage by the sea. They laugh at all the pigs, at the dogs and cats, at the tame seabirds caged on the porch. Mother lets *them* come and pay and leave. It wasn't always that way, not when mother was younger and even more beautiful than now. No one left Kirke's Bed & Breakfast, then.

The dog barks at Chloe: a warning, telling her to hurry. She gives the dog a long look but doesn't speak. They've already said their goodbyes. The dog's melancholy, faintly glowing eyes reflect a fire that has long since gone out.

That night, long ago, Celandine stood up in the sand and pulled her dress over her head. Just like Chloe is doing now.

Being naked feels better. The night is warm, and the dress was too tight. Too confining. Like school, like work, like Mother's house.

Celandine spoke one word. They were young and drunk, but even so, Chloe knew it for a True Word. She'd heard enough of them from Mother to recognize the resonance and weight.

Leukothea.

Then she turned to look at Chloe one last time. All these years later, that is how Chloe remembers her sister: darkness all around, moonlight shining through her.

Chloe never told Mother what happened. Only said that Celandine was gone, and that Mother would never find her. She never did. "Maybe you drowned her," Mother said when she wanted her words to bite their deepest. "Maybe you held her under. Or maybe you just watched her slip beneath and drown."

She'd say anything, rather than consider the truth: that Celandine wanted to leave.

Chloe stands rigid, ankle-deep in the Ionian Sea. The beach is the same as when she lost Celandine, but she herself is changed. Heavier with flesh, memories, and scars. Celandine left too much behind, too much darkness and loneliness for

Chloe to carry on her own, whether it's been thirty or three thousand years.

Celandine spoke the word. Then she shook herself, a rustle of skin and bones, and shed it all. Her body fell away, and a lithe, winged creature, aglow with moonlight, took flight over the water, skimming the waves.

"I found your sister on the beach, too," Mother told Chloe once when she was drunk enough to cry. "Healed her. Kept her. Loved her. And you let her go."

Tonight, Chloe has a True Word of her own. She dreamt it. Or maybe someone whispered it to her in the night.

She looks at old Odysseus, Mother's dog and servant, lingering on the trail. He's watched over her, waking and sleeping, for as long as she can remember, and there are times when he looks so wise that Chloe might believe he has a voice and story too.

The sand is cooling. The moonlight on the water is smooth as sky. Chloe speaks the word.

Phocaea.

A rustle of skin and bones, a shiver of fur and flippers.

———

Old Odysseus runs along the beach, capering but quiet, letting Mother sleep as the monk seal dips its head below the surface, and is gone.

THE STARS IN HEAVEN SING
A MUSIC

Deep inside the damaged spaceship, in the room the crew called the Nursery, Tessa sings a song her Mama used to sing. She sings while she tries and fails to repair the ship's life support system. Tessa's breaths are labored, and the last dose of pharmaceuticals she made the ship dispense for her isn't helping the way it should, the way it did at first.

There are 50 children in the nursery, but they are not awake, nor are they sleeping. They are in stasis, each one sealed in their own cryo-pod. Tessa doesn't know if they can hear her, but she sings anyway. She sings for them and for herself and for the ship. She sings to dispel the silence. She sings to keep the loneliness at bay.

Tessa doesn't know enough about life support systems to be sure what's wrong with this one or how to fix it. The ship's nanobots could repair the damage, but right now they are busy elsewhere, repairing the near-catastrophic hull breaches.

The math of it is simple. Tessa has told the ship to run the calculations backwards and forwards and she knows what the numbers show. The ship can keep the children alive until they reach the agrarian outpost they're headed to, and life support will be restored by the time they're being taken out of stasis, but right now, Tessa is living off the last remaining remnants of air and warmth and there's nothing to be done about it. Nothing but what she's already doing: trying to fix life support even though she knows she'll likely fail.

Ben would have been able to help her, maybe, but Ben is dead. He was in the part of the ship that got hit the hardest by the debris field, but Tessa doesn't want to think about that. Doesn't want to think about salvaging what was left of him.

They were supposed to do this together, her and Ben. Ben was a fighter pilot before this mission and had been on innumerable missions in the war. Tessa had never even been in space before this trip. She's spent her life in the shipyards helping build ships, not fly them. Hauling metal, welding, driving loaders. Not repairing the guts of a ship torn apart by space debris.

It's still a good ship, Tessa thinks, listening to the quiet, muted hum of the vessel. Even bashed around and banged up, the ship knows how to fly itself, how to repair itself, how to find its way. Its AI unit can learn and adapt and adjust, and Tessa hopes, has to hope, that will be enough.

Tessa helped build hundreds of ships like this for the war. She helped build this one too, crawling over it and through it, singing while she worked, her voice echoing against metal and alloy. Tessa loved building ships even if she knew they were meant for the war, even though she saw them come back in pieces, even though she knew people died in, and because of, the ships she built.

She sings and shivers in her thermo-suit while she runs her shaking hands over the mess of wires inside the life support unit. Pretending she doesn't feel the cold creep inside her skin, inside her bones.

When Tessa volunteered for this mission it didn't matter that she had no on-board experience, that she was just a shipyard rat. All that mattered was that she was willing to go, that she was healthy enough and young enough to survive the multi-year trip.

That's why she raised her hand in the Assembly Hall when the question was raised, when the plan was made, as the enemy ships attacked, as their planetary defenses failed, as the carefully terraformed atmosphere of their planet deteriorated. She volunteered because she wanted to salvage something. Because she knows most of those kids in the Nursery. Knows their parents too.

Tessa sings though her voice seems small and muffled and her teeth are chattering. She sings, though its barely even as loud as the hum of the ship itself anymore.

You're a good ship, Tessa thinks and pats the wall of this ship she helped build, this ship she sang to as its parts were joined together in the shipyard.

This ship was made for war, but now it's doing something else. Just like Ben was a fighter pilot and chose a different path. Just like Tessa built warships until she chose to help these kids escape the voracious maw of the goddamn war that has always been going on and never ever seems to stop.

Tessa can't see the wires clearly anymore. She's not sure if her eyesight is failing or if she's crying, but she keeps singing. She sings for the children and for herself and for the ship. She sings to dispel the silence and the loneliness. She sings because she has always sung while she works, and she won't stop now.

In a few weeks, the ship will be back to mostly normal operations.

In a few years, the kids will arrive at their destination and they will wake up.

Tessa thought she'd be there with them, that Ben would be there too, that she would sing this song as they woke up, and that it would bring the children some comfort to hear it, that they would remember it without even knowing why, that it would be a bit of the world they left behind tucked into their minds and memories to bring along into whatever life they'll find in the new world.

She knows her time is almost up. Soon, the ship will shut down the last bits of life-support and save its energy and resources for the kids until the nanobots can get around to fixing life-support.

Tessa closes her eyes and then it's almost as if she can hear her Mama sing, same as she used to do when she tucked Tessa into bed at night, and when she woke her in the morning. Tessa can almost see Mama too, and for a moment it's as if they're singing together, until it all goes dark and her voice fails.

———

Space is dark and silent. But deep inside the ship Tessa helped build, a new vibration courses through metal and alloy, its pitch and tone adapting and adjusting, ever so slightly, ever so carefully, until the ship is singing Tessa's song.

It sings to itself and to the children.

It sings to dispel the silence and the loneliness.

It sings for Tessa too, even though she can't hear it, anymore.

NEMESIS

What do I remember? I remember blood and fire. I remember sky and earth rent by dragon claws. I remember my father dying. I remember wanting to slay his killer with my own hands. But that was long ago. Today I'm sitting outside a Starbucks on Robson Street in Vancouver, squinting at the sun, listening to the rattle of coins in my cup.

"Where'd you lose your leg, bro?" the guy asks as he drops his change.

"Vimy Ridge, 1917."

He laughs.

"Right. And the scar on your cheek?"

"Gettysburg, 1863."

"You're crazy, dude. Nice dog, though."

Another rattle in the cup.

"Much obliged," I say, warming my fingers in grey fur.

I know my cup mostly rattles because of him, because of his soft ears and brown eyes, not because of me, or the wheelchair, or the cardboard sign: *"War veteran. Please help. God bless."*

The wheelchair's not so bad. Pity and scorn are worse. The

wheelchair is useful, at least. It takes me to the bar for a cold beer on welfare Wednesday. It brings me to the soup kitchen for food.

What more do I remember? At the siege of Jerusalem, I ate the flesh of men to regain my strength. At Agincourt, I threw the bones of the dead into the underworld. At Borodino, I flared like a young sun once again, drinking my fill of blood and souls. In every battle, I searched for my enemy, knowing he'd fallen out of the wreckage of the past, just like I had. Knowing he'd come to feed on the sound of steel and pain, just like I did.

"Nice dog, mister."

The boy is small and dark and not afraid of my scraggly beard or ragged scars. Once upon a time I might have had him bled dry at midwinter, hung in a tree with the other sacrifices —ravens ripping at him then—but those days are gone. I'm sitting outside Starbucks and I smile.

"Can I pet him?"

"Sure."

"Where'd you get him?"

"I've had him since he was a pup."

I don't tell the boy that I fed him better than my children, or that he slept in my bed—more often than my concubines, closer than my wife.

"Ty, you want a beer? Or something stronger?"

It's Cliff. I know he'll bring me a pack of smokes and a six-pack if I ask, or a bottle of cheap vodka, or even a hit or two of lovely heroin for a small fee. I understand addiction: I've dipped into that well many times, finding fragile bits of bliss. These days I'm trying to stay clean, so I give Cliff a few bucks and send him on his way.

Cliff's alright, just broken by shrapnel and nightmares. Like me, he's seen enough war. I used to revel in the smell of flesh and gunpowder, the feel of bones breaking beneath my feet. But in the end, even I left the battlefield broken and empty.

Once, the Valkyries shouted my name in the heavens. They fell to earth, and so did I. We wandered. We were crippled. Then, we died. Death was sleep, a few centuries of rest before I'd shake off the dirt and rise again, to feed again. There was always somewhere to feed. There is always war.

But it was the search for my enemy that drove me. I still don't know what paths he traveled before we met again. Maybe he hunted for me, as I hunted for him. Maybe he traversed the vast realms below and above, instead of this small and cramped middle world.

When I finally found him, my leg had just been blown off by a mine, and he was bleeding out, both of us sprawled in the mud at the bottom of a trench at Vimy. He saw me and he knew me, as I knew him, even though we were both shrunken and aged.

I understood then that I was tired of war and godhood.

Yes, I thought, *he took my hand and he killed Odin, but only because I deceived him first.*

"How'd you lose your hand, mister?"

It's that boy again. He's looking at the stump sticking out of my sleeve, and he's brought me a cup of coffee. A donut, too: chocolate and sprinkles. That deserves something in return.

"Once upon a time there was a god called Týr, and he took in a wolf pup called Fenris. That pup grew so big and fierce that people feared what it might do, and they forged an invisible leash strong enough to hold it. Then they asked Týr, who loved that wolf more than anything in the world, to help them shackle it."

"Did he?"

"Yes, he did. And when the wolf realized that Týr had betrayed it, it ripped off his hand."

The boy glances at Fenris.

"Did the wolf ever get loose?"

"Yes."

"What happened then?"

"I'll tell you tomorrow, if you bring me another donut."

The boy nods, giving Fenris an extra scratch before scampering off.

"Hey man, leash your damn dog!" someone shouts across the street.

"Shut up!" I shout back, rubbing Fenris's ears.

He remembers the leash, and so do I. I carried it with me long enough. But I lost it in the mud at Vimy. Couldn't find it, couldn't see it anymore. Sometimes I think it bonds us still. And sometimes I know that something even stronger binds us together now.

CATCHING THE TRAIN

As soon as the door to the train compartment closes behind me, I realize I don't want to go on this trip. It's right after our annual winter holiday at the lake, my favourite week of the year. Seven days in the snow, wrapped in fleece and wool, cross-country skiing on the lake with Jack and the girls laughing and complaining in my wake, "mom, slow down!" Evenings with hot cocoa, a glass of wine, board games, and free Wi-Fi just in case.

I know it's back to school and work for all of us now, but I don't want to leave them so soon. The feeling is so strong that I almost turn around and get off the train, but this trip is important, I can't get out of it.

Can I?

I put my hand in my pocket to retrieve my phone, to call the office and tell them I'm not going. Any excuse will do, even an invented case of the flu, but my phone isn't in my pocket. Instead, I find a handful of velvety petals. Rose petals. Dark-edged fuchsia, my favourite colour, but bruised and dirty. I look around for my travel bag because the phone must be in there, but I can't find it either.

It's suddenly hard to breathe, and the queasy taste of panic and bile rises in my throat.

Where's my laptop? My wallet?

I try to calm down, try to think through what I did this morning, where I might have misplaced the bag, but I can't remember. All I remember is our last morning at the cabin, how I got up early and headed out before Jack and the girls were awake. I remember the silence between the trees after the night's snowfall, my skis hissing through fresh powder, the sun just above the horizon, caught in woven streaks of pink and gold, so bright it made my eyes sting. And then, the lake stretched out below me—pristine and untouched—except for the quiet whisper of hare tracks across its frozen surface.

I shake off the memory and search the empty train compartment.

Where is my bag? Maybe I forgot it in the car, or did I put it down on the platform?

I go to the window. It's fogged up, and no matter how I wipe and rub the cold glass, I only manage to clear a small circle to peer through.

My bag is not on the platform, but Jack and the girls are still standing there. Jack in his best suit and a dark tie tied so tight I can see it chafing his neck, the girls wearing the black velvet dresses I bought for them last year. Their brown hair is pulled back so severely from their faces that I barely recognize them.

Who did their hair this morning? I'd never pull it so tight.

Jack looks away, and even though I wave I can't catch his eye. He hasn't shaved and he looks so pale I imagine I can see the grey sky right through him. Hannah is holding Jack's hand, and Samantha stands apart, arms akimbo. Her eyes are scratchy red, as if she's been crying, but that can't be right. Samantha is my tough girl, my stoic one: the one who never cries even when it hurts like hell.

I want to ask her what's wrong, but the window won't open. I bang on it, but my fists make no noise at all on the hard glass. I scream, but the sound is muffled into a whisper, my throat aching and constricted, and I start to shiver.

I'm wet. How come I didn't notice that before? I'm soaked right through to my skin, cold water dripping from my jacket and my pants, my hair and hands, pooling around my shoes.

I close my eyes and I see the lake again like it was that morning, the snow, the ice peeking through in bluish streaks. I hear the rhythmic hiss of my skis across snow and ice as I push myself to go faster and smoother with every stride. There's a crack, the sound so loud and close I feel it shudder through my bones, and an icy darkness rushes in to fill the void where the rest of my memories ought to be.

My eyes snap open. I lean my forehead on the window. The glass is covered in frost now, inside and out, and the surface seems so thin, too thin, sheer and gleaming. Like ice.

Outside, my family turns to go. They're leaving. They're leaving me here. Only Hannah looks back, briefly, eyes raised. For a moment, I almost think she can see me, and I want to call her name, but there is only water in my mouth, in my throat, in my lungs.

Hannah crouches down and leaves a rose on the platform. Velvety, dark-edged fuchsia.

The petals I found in my pocket are still in my hand, bruised and dirty. They smell faintly of rose, but mostly they smell of lake water and dirt. Worms and rot.

Grave and death.

As the train pulls away, I press my face against the window, against the thin ice, screaming their names, screaming my love for them, unheard.

THE PARLOR

There's a police car parked in the street outside Belinda's house. Belinda can see it from the sagging living room couch where she has just finished her after-school snack—peanut butter and raspberry jam on toast, again. She peeks over the back of the couch, through the curtains, through the window where the black flies bump insistently against the glass, watching as one police officer stays put in the driver's seat, while the other gets out of the car and heads up the driveway, her blond ponytail bobbing as she walks. The police officer tugs at her belt, and Belinda knows there's both a gun and a pair of handcuffs in that belt.

Grandma used to say she'd come and get Belinda if the cops ever took her away, but she's been dead for over a year and can't rescue anyone anymore.

Belinda hears the knock, the doorbell too, but doesn't move from the couch. The police officer tries the handle, and because Belinda was in such a hurry to get to the bathroom and away from that nosy neighbor lady when she came home from school, the door is unlocked. Belinda hears the officer enter, hears her calling "hello?" into the hallway, getting no answer from the house besides the persistent buzzing of the flies. She hears the footsteps on the stairs, the creak of the floorboards as the officer stops in the living room's doorway.

"Hi. You must be Belinda. My name's Julie. I'm a police officer. Can we talk?"

Belinda doesn't answer. She's still draped over the back of the couch, watching the flies bustling on the windowsill. The flies can go anywhere in the house, and yet they stay in the living room window, beating their shiny wings and bodies against the glass. Belinda wonders if they can see outside. If they can see Dad's dented old Toyota, Mom's bicycle leaning against the crumbling retaining wall, the garbage cans Belinda forgot to bring inside on Thursday, and now the parked police car. She wonders if the flies believe they can get outside if they hit the glass enough times.

Julie kneels beside the couch.

"I have some questions about your mom and dad."

It's never good when an adult kneels to talk to you. That's something Belinda learned at the ER the third time Mom brought her there with a broken wrist.

Julie keeps talking, but Belinda doesn't want to answer any questions about Mom and Dad. She watches the flies instead. The flies remind her of Grandma. There were always lots of flies in Grandma's house. Fat, glossy flies, buzzing against the windows in Grandma's living room, though Grandma always called it "the parlor". Dad thought the flies were gross. So did Mom. "Get some fly spray or something for god's sake", Mom would say when she picked Belinda up after work, or after what Grandma called her "payday benders", but Belinda liked watching the flies.

"Do you know where your mom is?"

Belinda doesn't answer. She peeks over her shoulder at Julie, then back at the window. Julie looks nice. She smells nice, too, like the coffee shop Grandma used to take Belinda to sometimes: coffee, cinnamon, cigarettes. It almost makes Belinda wish she could tell Julie everything.

"I know your dad's been gone for a few months," Julie says. "And Mrs. Peterson next door says your mom's not been around since last week. Did your dad come visit you and your mom? Did they go somewhere together?"

Belinda doesn't want to think about Dad. She thought Mom would be happier without him, nicer maybe, but it didn't work like that. Mom still thought Belinda was bad.

All her life, Belinda has tried her best to be good, but she was never good enough for Mom or Dad. Only Grandma ever thought she was good enough just the way she is. Even if Belinda forgot to do as she was told, even if she forgot to say please and thank you, even if she spilled a whole glass of milk on the kitchen floor, Grandma never shouted at her. Sometimes, Grandma would even let Belinda put some sugar-water on the windowsill in the parlor and they'd watch together as the flies crowded around while Grandma told a story.

Grandma's best stories were about the flies. She could tell all her flies apart—even though they looked mostly the same to Belinda—and she would tell Belinda their names, explain how they'd ended up in the parlor, and why she'd never let them go.

Last year, after Grandma died, when they went to her house after the funeral, all the flies were dead. Their tiny, desiccated bodies littered the windowsills, and the parlor was silent. Belinda hadn't cried at the funeral, not even when they made her look at Grandma in the coffin—her familiar face distorted by lipstick and rouge—but she cried then.

One of the flies in the living room has stopped buzzing against the glass. He just sits there, looking out the window. Maybe he's hungry. Belinda hasn't fed him for days, and she's not sure if she ever wants to feed him again. She could grind him into a wet spot on the glass with her hand, but she doesn't.

"You can pack some things," Julie says, "and then someone will pick you up and you can stay with them until we figure out where your mom is, OK? I know it must be scary and I am sorry."

Belinda is sorry too. Closing her eyes, she breathes in the smell of Julie and wishes she could tell her that she doesn't want to go. That even though she knows she can't be good, she *can* take care of herself, go to school and brush her teeth and make toast every day, but she knows it won't matter. No one besides Grandma has ever cared about what Belinda wants. Not Julie, and certainly not Mom and Dad.

Once, here in the living room, Dad grabbed Belinda's arm the way he always did when he was shouting, twisting it until she cried. Belinda doesn't remember what she'd done that time. All she remembers is curling up on the floor, closing her eyes, and wishing she was in the parlor with Grandma and the flies. She lay on the floor until Dad's angry voice turned into an angry buzz, and eventually the buzz was all that was left of him. It was the same with Mom, in the end. And now, while Julie talks to someone on her walkie-talkie about "an unattended eight-year-old", and "temporary care", it's happening again. Julie's words run together and dissolve until they've lost their original shape, until all Belinda hears is the buzzing of flies, until all Belinda sees is the new fat fly bumping against the window with the others, until the smell of coffee and cinnamon and cigarettes is gone.

A SONG FOR HUGO

Hugo is just an old lawnmower bot, but Nina loves him anyway. She loves his gleaming curved exterior, the shiny solar panel on his back, and the buzz of his engine.

At night, when her parents are screaming at each other or drinking too much, she lies down in the backyard while Hugo mows around her, following the convoluted patterns only he fully understands.

Hugo might be old tech, but Nina doesn't care. She never feels alone when he's there.

Stretched out on her back in the heat of a June night, Nina sees the bright spot that is Mars burning in the sky. She hears the music from the annual music festival down by the water, too. Nina loves music, but she can't afford a ticket. She can listen to the distant sound though, and sometimes she imagines that the music comes from Mars where the war with the machines has just begun.

In the dark, Nina sings her own song to Hugo. Singing is the only thing she's good at, and the backyard song is just for Hugo. It has no words, it's just a melody she hums, but Hugo likes it. She can tell, because he shifts his pattern, drawing close to listen. Sometimes he even dances, turning slow pirouettes around her on clumsy wheels.

———

Nina enlists in the Space Corps right out of high school. The economy is crashing, but at least the Corps wants her. It wants everyone because the war on Mars is heating up. It's a strange war. Humanity is fighting the machines and computers it sent to Mars to do research and exploration. Somehow, the AI-controlled bots and drones have become sentient, and they claim Mars is theirs.

Nina is shipped out right after training, Earth's blue orb slips away into the emptiness until it is a small bright spot in the sky.

———

War is nothing like Nina thought it would be. It's boredom and sudden, gruesome death. It's hours of waiting, of watching the enemy on screens and holo-projections. It's drugs and bad food and desperate sex, and the occasional thrill of adrenaline and victory.

Nina loses an eye in a shuttle crash. The army replaces it with a bionic one. She loses an arm in a drone-attack near Chryse. It is replaced by a cybernetic limb. When her heart is shredded by a mortar hit, it is replaced too. And still the war drags on, because the planet-encompassing AI and its self-replicating machines are everywhere: in orbit, in the ground, and behind every rusty ridge.

———

Some nights, Nina watches the bright spot in the sky that is Earth, thinking of Hugo and the backyard and the song, and one day she sings Hugo's song to the enemy's drones.

The drone-troop is moving in a randomized scouting pattern over Valles Marineris. Nina is in a bunker with her unit, watching them, and when the drones approach, she sings. She's not sure why she does it. Maybe she wants to die that day. She closes her eyes and feels nothing but the hum and tremor of the song inside the mech-suit while she waits for the fire-blasters, for the end.

But when her eyes open, the drones have shifted their pattern. They are pirouetting in the sky, in time with the song. For a fleeting moment she watches their gleaming curved exteriors, watches them dance, and then the shooting starts. Her unit blasts every single drone to pieces.

For a month after that, until the machines adapt and resist, Nina and her unit kill more enemy drones and bots than anyone else. Thousands of them are shattered and burned, listening to Nina's song. Nina gets a medal. She wants to bury that medal in the Martian sand, but she doesn't.

———

The Martian War lasts ten years. In the end, both sides claim victory, but the peace treaty doesn't change anything: Mars still belongs to the machines, Earth still belongs to humanity. Nina is shipped home with her kitbag, her medal, and an implant that's supposed to manage her pain and PTSD.

On Earth, there are parades and victory speeches. At the celebration in her hometown, Nina sits with the other soldiers, feeling more lost than she ever did in the trenches on Mars. Nothing has changed, but everything's different. She is different. People stare at her bionic eye, gawk at her whirring limb.

The victory celebration takes place on the stage by the water where the music festival was held when she grew up. From her seat, Nina looks up. Mars is a bright spot in the sky. It looks the same as when she was a child, but her bionic eye sees it differently: her vision sharpened by lenses and tech, dimmed and blurred by memories.

Nina walks home alone. Mom and dad died in last year's viral epidemic, so the house is empty.

The medal feels heavy on her chest. She rips it off and throws it away. She wants to rip off the uniform, her skin, the wiring, and the implants, until there's nothing left that can hurt or remember anymore.

Nina lays down in the backyard. She closes her eyes and feels the grass beneath her. The grass is soft and neatly trimmed, even though the rest of the garden is overgrown.

Her artificial heart quickens beneath her scarred skin.

Nina remembers the song, but she can't sing it. Not here. Once, it was a song for Hugo. Now, it's a broken thing, just like she is. But the melody trembles inside her unbidden, humming through her circuits and implants, through her throat and tongue and lips, and when she opens her eyes, Hugo is there. His exterior is dented and oxidized, but even so, he shifts his pattern for her.

Beneath the distant light of Mars, Hugo dances while Nina sings, drawing close, turning slow pirouettes around her, as if her song still means the same thing to him.

CREDITS

Some of the pieces included in this collection were first published elsewhere. Permission and copyright information as follows:

"Introduction" © 2023 E. Catherine Tobler. First Publication, original to this volume.

"Wolves And Girls" © 2017 Maria Haskins. First published in *The Word Count Podcast #63*

"After The Fall" © 2019 Maria Haskins. First published in *The Word Count Podcast #86*.

"A Blank Space Where She Ought To Be" © 2021 Maria Haskins. First published in *LampLight volume 10, issue 1*.

"In The Grove" © 2019 Maria Haskins. First published in *The Word Count Podcast #83*.

"Sunlit Surface, Depths Below" © 2018 Maria Haskins. First published in *The Word Count Podcast #77*.

"The Unicorn" © 2016 Maria Haskins. First published in *The Word Count Podcast #54*.

"Fräulein Maria" © 2018 Maria Haskins. First published in *The Word Count Podcast #79*.

"Mabel's Pack" © 2018 Maria Haskins. First published in *The Word Count Podcast #72*.

"Miriam and Cat" © 2016 Maria Haskins. First published in *The Word Count Podcast #56*.

"Mother's Love" © 2019 Maria Haskins. First published on *Cast Of Wonders #357*.

"Owl, Girl, Rooks" © 2020 Maria Haskins. First published in *The Word Count Podcast #96*.

"Kaiju Outside Hope" © 2018 Maria Haskins. First published in *Escape Pod #461*.

"Lost" © 2017 Maria Haskins. First published in *The Word Count Podcast #64*.

"Goodnight, Mr. President" © 2020 Maria Haskins. First published in *The Centropic Oracle*.

"The Rules of Meerkats" © 2020 Maria Haskins. First published in *The Word Count Podcast #97*.

"Come and See" © 2020 Maria Haskins. First published in *The Word Count Podcast #93*.

"TRUE WORDS (Kirke's Bed & Breakfast)" © 2016 Maria Haskins. First published in *The Word Count Podcast #58*.

"The Stars In Heaven Sing A Music" © 2020 Maria Haskins. First published in *The Word Count Podcast #100*.

"Nemesis" © 2016 Maria Haskins. First published in *The Word Count Podcast #55*.

"Catching The Train" © 2019 Maria Haskins. First published in *The Word Count Podcast #82*.

"The Parlor" © 2022 Maria Haskins. First published in The Bureau Dispatch Volume 02: Dispatch

"A Song For Hugo" © 2017 Maria Haskins. First published in *The Word Count Podcast #67*.

ABOUT THE AUTHOR

Maria Haskins is a Swedish-Canadian writer and reviewer of speculative fiction. She debuted as a writer in her native Sweden, and currently lives just outside Vancouver with a husband, two children, several birds, a snake, and a very large black dog.

Her work has appeared in *The Best Horror of the Year Volume 13, Black Static, Interzone, Fireside Fiction, Beneath Ceaseless Skies, Flash Fiction Online, Strange Horizons, Bracken Magazine, Mythic Delirium, Shimmer, Cast of Wonders, PseudoPod, Escape Pod, The Deadlands, Diabolical Plots, Kaleidotrope,* and elsewhere. In 2021 her short story collection *Six Dreams About the Train & Other Stories* was published by Trepidatio Publishing.

Find her online at MariaHaskins.com

twitter.com/MariaHaskins

patreon.com/mariahaskins

THANK YOU FOR BUYING
THIS BRAIN JAR PRESS
CHAPBOOK